EARTH SHATTERING

ST. LEASING – BOOK 6

L.P. Maxa

ALSO BY L.P. MAXA

RiffRaff Records
Royalty
Legacy
Infamy
Loyalty
Sanctuary
Piracy
Certainty
Inevitably
Finally

The Devil's Share
Play Nice
Play Dirty
Play Fair
Play Softly
Play Hard
Play For Keeps

St. Leasing
Mouth Watering
Breath Taking
Jaw Dropping
Heart Stopping
Soul Crushing

Other Novels

Happy Place
Stumbled into Love
Rescued
The Forever Weekend
The Ideal

www.BOROUGHSPUBLISHINGGROUP.com

EARTH SHATTERING
Copyright © 2021 L.P. Maxa

ISBN: 978-1-953810-59-5

To my new, larger, family
I'm beyond grateful you've come into existence

ACKNOWLEDGMENTS

Thank you to BOTH my beautiful daughters for hanging out with your way more fun dad so I could work. This book was hard to find space for. I wrote it in the middle of a pandemic, in the middle of a home study, in the middle of an adoption. There was so much on my mind, all the time. But it was all a labor of love, *Earth Shattering* included. Our baby girl's first mom named her Riley. And it's so fitting that the first book I wrote after she came into our world was this one. Riley (boy Riley) was the first young character I created.

Thank you to all my readers for your support over the last year. I can't explain how much it means to me. There are no words. You rooted for me and my family. You were excited for us, you cried happy tears for us. I am eternally grateful.

EARTH SHATTERING

"Love is friendship that has caught fire."
– Ann Landers

PART ONE
THE LIES
Riley

Chapter One

Loneliness wasn't something new. Riley had been an only child with an absentee father and working mom for the majority of his life. When his mother married his stepdad, so many things about both of their lives had changed. He'd gained a big extended family, and he'd been sent to St. Leasing, a private school for shifters like himself and his stepdad. He'd spent four years at the private school nestled in the mountain forest outside the tiny Colorado town of Haxton. There, he'd met his best friend Jasper. And there, through a series of dramatic events, he'd become part of a pack. A true wolf pack. Hell, they even had an alpha and beta.

He'd woken after his first night in his new dorm room and realized he was alone for the first time in over four years. Back in Haxton, he'd had his teammates, his friends, his roommates. He had Dom and Corey, who were like an odd hybrid of surrogate parents and cool older siblings. And he had Hadley, his cosmic little sister, whom he worshipped. Riley had always wanted siblings, and the universe had delivered in a big way. Not only did he consider Jasper and Jace his brothers, but he had Hadley now too. He was nervous when he found out that destiny had chosen him to play the part of her big brother, her protector. He couldn't imagine his life without her though. He was surrounded, constantly, by the people he loved and they loved him in return.

Since coming to the University of Northern Colorado to play baseball, lonely was all he'd felt. There was no Jasper to encourage devious choices. There was no broody Jace tossing a laughing Axie over his shoulder to take her upstairs so he didn't fuck her on the kitchen counter. No Corey to watch trashy TV with. No Dom to go on late night runs with. Don't even get him started on the hole in his chest where Hadley belonged. He missed his pack, every single one of them. He even missed Linc and his constantly inappropriate humor.

Riley turned the music up on his AirPods, trying like hell to drown out the party going strong in the hallway outside his dorm room. He wanted to get through the next couple weeks, and then get back to Haxton for Christmas with his family. He didn't want to drink warm keg beer with the other freshmen from his floor. He didn't want to wrap a sheet around his body and call it a nod to the Greeks. He didn't want to hook up with some random chick in her attempt to give zero fucks about the guy who'd ghosted her earlier in the day.

It'd been four months since he moved to the University of Northern Colorado by himself, and sure he'd been back to Haxton for visits, but he was more than ready for this fall semester to be over. He was ready for Jasper to come join him in Greenly. He was ready to have at least a small part of his pack with him for the everyday stuff. For breakfast in the dining hall, for practice, and for classes. He hated feeling like a pussy, but he needed his best friend.

Baseball season was starting soon, and Riley knew his reclusive existence would no longer be tolerated by his new coaches or by his teammates. It was already hard enough turning down their constant invites, but when it became more about team building and less about getting to know you bullshit, he'd be out of excuses. The thought of making new friends, of building a new team around him, almost made him ill. It made the ache in his chest for his real pack unbearable. But at least by then, Jasper would be here with him.

"Hey, can I use your bathroom?" Riley whirled around, his eyes gone wide as his door was thrown open so hard it hit the wall. "Thanks." He'd turned from his desk in time to see a mass of bubblegum pink sheets trail into the bathroom.

Who does that? Who walks into someone else's room and uses their bathroom without waiting for permission?

He stood from his desk, shoving a pencil behind his ear. He heard the toilet flush, then the faucet come on. Well, at least whoever they were washed their damn hands.

No one came into his room unannounced. He didn't have the same no-locks policy the rest of the co-ed floor did. And he was more than irritated that someone had the balls to come in like it wasn't a complete invasion of his privacy. He'd been wallowing in self-pity and they'd interrupted.

When the door opened moments later, he made sure he was wearing his most annoyed scowl with his arms crossed over his chest, channeling Baze and Jace as best he could. "Uh, hello?" He used Axie's snarky tone too.

"Hey, thanks." Blonde curls bounced into view as the girl who'd barged into his room dipped down to gather the extra yards of pink fabric hanging from her petite frame. "I had to go so bad and the line for the one down the hall was intense." She stood up straight, holding her sheets over her arm.

Even at her full height—maybe five-three—she was petite and unimposing. Her hair was the color of a wheat field, framing her face and making her cornflower blue eyes appear even bluer. She was pretty. Well fuck it, she was gorgeous. She was studying him with humor in her gaze and a smirk on her glossy pink lips. He had no clue what she could possibly find funny about this invasion.

"Do I know you?" He wouldn't let her good mood obliterate his sour one.

She cocked her head to the side, her curls falling over her bare collarbone. "Do you know anyone?"

Riley jerked back, annoyed she had the balls to ask him that question. Why would a tiny blonde wearing a bubblegum pink sheet be standing in his dorm room calling him on his bullshit?

He decided to stand his ground, going for intimidating, but she didn't cower. He reached deep, pulling out a bit of his shifter magic, putting menacing vibes in the air designed to scare her away. But she didn't back out of the room mumbling an apology like he'd expected.

No, instead she stepped closer, trailing her fingertips over the smooth surface of his dresser. "Why are you in here?" She jerked her thumb behind her. "The party is out there."

"Thus, the reason I'm in here." He took a deep breath, puffing out his chest even farther. He was trying his damnedest to make her feel uncomfortable, but it didn't seem to be working.

She nodded, making her hair swing around her bare shoulders. "Oh. You're one of those people who don't like fun?" Her toga was wrapped tight around her chest, showing off her curves. He might be annoyed as fuck by her presence, but he wasn't blind.

"Wearing a sheet and drinking cheap beer isn't my idea of a good time." He was still standing, still rigid, still mentally trying to make her leave his safe space. "You can go now." He made a shooing motion toward the door.

The blonde laughed lightly, the sound filling the air around him like an intrusive song. "Did you really just dismiss me?" She waved her hands down her body. "I'm standing in your room wearing a thin sheet, three beers in. Flirting. And you shooed me?"

He raised one eyebrow, not letting himself smile even though her incredulous tone was almost making him want to. "Are you asking me why I'm not hitting on you? A female I've never met before, who, by her own admission, is under the influence of alcohol. Really?"

Was she asking him to take advantage of her? That was fucking insane.

Her lips pursed, her eyes narrowing slightly. "Good point."

"So again." He shooed her. "You can go."

She didn't leave, she moved closer still. She was standing a couple feet away from him, her sweet scent wrapping around him. She was wearing pink and she smelled like candy; he didn't know if he should laugh or physically shove her out of his room. Riley wasn't into chicks like this. Chicks who looked like they belonged in some boy band's music video. All highlights and smiles on shiny lips. She didn't fit his current morose personality, and he didn't want anyone trying to bring him out of his funk.

"No, I think I'll stay." She lifted her chin, defying him. "You look like you need a friend."

"I don't." He had friends. He had a whole damn pack. "Thanks, though."

"You always like this?" She launched past him, jumping onto his twin-size mattress, her sheets fluttering with the movement. "Moody and rude?"

He sighed at that question, because he wasn't. He was usually a really nice guy. Pleasant and easy to get along with. He was kind to the people he cared about, and he went out of his way to make others happy. But over the course of this semester, he'd been discourteous and utterly distant. He hadn't given anyone a chance to get to know him, preferring to soak in his sadness, feeling sorry for himself, and regretting his decision to come here without Jasper.

"No." The chick on his bed was nosy and she couldn't seem to take a hint, but she was trying to befriend him. He could at least be polite about shoving her out of his room. Corey would be appalled at him shooing her like pigeon. Jasper would kick his ass for turning away a flirty chick wearing next to nothing. "No, I'm not."

She nodded, pulling her hair up into a ponytail at the top of her skull, her curls bouncing. "Why so blue, boo?"

He gave up and cracked a smile at that, taking a seat at his desk. Where he was before she so rudely interrupted him. "I guess, I uh, I miss my family." She blinked at him, her dark lashes fanning her face. Her expectant gaze was making him feel like his admission wasn't enough for her. "I've never really been away from them." He'd never been away from his pack, never been away from Jasper since they'd started together at St. Leasing as freshmen.

"Are you away from them now?" She sat up, reaching to his desk and picking up the framed picture Corey had given him before he'd pulled out of their driveway four months ago.

It was everyone, the whole pack. He was cradling Hadley to his chest, with Jasper's arm slung around his shoulders. Corey was next to him, Dom standing behind like he was watching over his girls. Jace and Axie only had eyes for each other, per the norm. Linc had said something that made Madden laugh with her head thrown back. His hand was on her rounded stomach. Keller and Molly were smiling like they had a secret, and Baze and Penn were clinging to each other and Jace's shoulders. Every time Riley looked at that pic he felt equal parts happy and sad.

"Because it seems to me, you're still there with them." The pretty stranger put his picture back down, her gaze searching his. "When is the last time you had fun, sourpuss?"

He chuckled, humorlessly. "Couldn't tell you."

Although if he had a gun to his head, which wasn't an unreasonable exaggeration given the life he'd lived back in Haxton, it was a few nights before he left home. He, Jace, and Jasper had gone to Moon Bar for drinks. The rest of the pack had surprised him with a going-away party; all his favorite people were there. They drank and danced, and laughed. They had cake. He and Jasper had shared a waitress at their borrowed apartment, the perfect going-away night.

"Well. It's a good thing I really needed to pee, huh?" The girl gathered her sheet, hopping off his neatly made bed. "Come on, let's teach you how it feels to smile again."

He crossed his arms back over his chest, instantly uncomfortable at the thought of leaving his room. It was as if he was afraid to shed his sadness. Like he wasn't entirely sure who he'd be here without it. "I don't even know you."

She held out her hand. "I'm Blake." When he didn't immediately offer her his palm, she reached down and took it without permission. Shaking it with a smirk on her face. "This is the part where you tell me your name. Unless you want me to keep calling you sourpuss all night."

"Riley." He took a deep breath, letting her pull him to his feet, towering over her once he was standing. He suddenly decided he liked the feel of her small hand in his, and he liked he was bigger than her. He liked the way she was all light and sweet, infusing his veins with happiness even when he'd tried to deny her. She wasn't scared of him. No way was she intimidated.

She should've been. She'd made friends with a wolf, and she had no fucking clue. Blake had no sense of self-perseveration, no sixth sense that alerted her to danger. He found himself wanting to protect her, if only for the night.

She dropped his palm. "Well, we've got to find me something else to wear then, huh?" She whirled around, going to his closet, throwing open the double doors to the wardrobe like she had every right. "I'm sure you've got something that'll resemble a dress on me." She winked at him over her shoulder. "You're massive."

He smirked, starting to feel more like his old self than he had in months. "You have no idea."

She let out a dramatic gasp. "Did you make a joke? Holy crap, I didn't know you had it in you."

She was right. He'd almost forgotten how to make a joke, how to smile and laugh. He'd been half of a person away from his pack, away from his family. Maybe this bubblegum pink firecracker was what he needed right now. Someone to demand he have fun, someone to not take no for an answer.

Maybe Blake could help him survive the next few weeks, and then after that, Jasper would be moving in and everything would feel right again.

Chapter Two

Riley sat up, groaning at the incessant dinging coming from the floor beside his bed. He peered over the side, snatching up his cell, which had somehow fallen. He tried to swallow, but his throat was dry as hell and sore. He uncapped the bottle of water sitting on his nightstand, draining it in a few gulps. His head was pounding, but getting out of bed to search for medicine was not about to happen. He was hung over, which meant he'd basically drank the bar dry. He was a shifter. He was of another world. It took a hell of a lot of alcohol for him to be hurting the next day. Usually, his healing sleep would take care of the headaches and grogginess.

He clicked his cell open, noting that it was barely eight o'clock in the morning. He'd only been asleep for five hours. No wonder he still felt like shit. He needed to go back to bed. He needed the wolf inside him to do its damn job and heal them both.

His phone pinged again, reminding him of what had woken him up in the first place.

Blake: Morning sourpuss, I wanted to make sure your body survived your first college party last night. I know that much of a good time can be taxing.

Blake: Hey. Wake up.

Blake: Are you dead? If you're dead, it wasn't my fault.

Blake: Shit. I'm going to have to come steal your cell and erase these messages if you're dead. I've basically incriminated myself as the means of your demise.

Blake: Is your door unlocked? Maybe I can YouTube lock picking?

Blake. The demanding girl who had burst into his room wearing a pink sheet and all but forced him to be her friend. Some friend she was. He was pretty sure she was the one pouring vodka down his throat last night. She'd dragged him to a bar a few blocks off campus, they'd danced, and she knew everyone. They'd drunk for free, and then they'd stumbled back to campus eating cheap tacos. He'd walked her home, and then he'd weaved his way to his own dorm, promptly passing out.

Riley: Morning Barbie Doll. I lived. No thanks to you. What the hell was in those drinks you made me?

Blake: Little of this, little of that. And Barbie Doll?

Riley: Big blue eyes and blonde curls, you look like a tiny Barbie Doll. Little of this, little of that? Isn't that what douche bags say before they roofie people?

Blake: Funny. What are you doing? Brooding in your room wearing all black?

He looked down, picking up his comforter. He wasn't really wearing much of anything, although his boxer briefs were actually black.

Riley: I am wearing black. But I'm not brooding, I was sleeping. I don't have to be up for another few hours for weight training with the team. See? I leave my room.

Blake: When it's mandated by your coaches.

Riley: And apparently when bubbly strangers hijack my bathroom.

Blake: My bitchy roommate is here with her gross emo boyfriend. If I have to listen to them coo at each other for another minute I'll die. I'm coming to hang with you.

He chuckled at her dramatics. Blake seemed to tackle everything with all she had: meeting people, dancing, drinking, conversations.

Riley: Forcing yourself into my life again so soon?

Blake: Force? Nah. You need me sourpuss. I'm basically saving your boring ass life.

Riley: I can assure you, my life is anything but boring.

Blake: Well now it's not, I'm your new bestie.

He didn't need a new bestie, but telling her that wouldn't make a difference. Blake had decided that they were going to be friends, and he knew from last night arguing wouldn't deter her.

He lay back on his pillows, staring at the white popcorn ceiling. Going out with her had been fun. He'd laughed, he'd danced, he'd drunk enough to drown a fish. He supposed that having a friend at UNC wouldn't be the worst thing in the world.

Riley: Door's open doll face.

Chapter Three

Why did all his mornings seem to be starting the same way? Him lying in bed, being woken up by the incessant pinging of his cell phone. Blake didn't seem to need sleep like the average human. She was always full of energy, always looking for the next adventure to drag him to. It had been a week since they'd meet, a week since she'd barged into his room and demanded his compliance as her ever-present accomplice.

He had to admit, he felt lighter. He was happier. He was actually enjoying college for the first time since he'd gotten here four months ago. The only thing giving him pause was knowing Jasper was going to definitely try to nail Blake once he moved onto campus. She was gorgeous and flirty. She'd be able to keep up with his sarcastic innuendos. In short, she was fucking catnip for Jasper, and a juicy bone for his wolf. It wasn't jealousy causing him concern. He knew Blake was a fucking snack, and she'd made his dick hard as stone on more than one occasion. But she wasn't for him. She wasn't his forever. So what was the point in pursuing her? He'd end up losing her as a friend, and the thought made his chest ache.

Jasper? He'd have no issue severing a blossoming friendship in order to get his dick wet. That was a problem for another day he supposed. He couldn't seem to shake her, and there was still a whole Christmas vacation before Jasper would be gracing the UNC campus with his larger-than-life presence.

Blake: *I think I died.*
Always so dramatic.

Riley: So, on a level of one to a hundred, how bad is your hangover?

Blake: One hundred, for sure. What the hell happened last night? It went from let's go play pool, to stop dancing on the bar, Barbie.

He laughed to himself because he definitely had to make her get off the bar. She was performing for everyone, *Coyote Ugly*-style. Her blonde hair was swinging, and bodies were packing in tighter and tighter to see the show. Riley had plucked her off the slippery surface moments before she faceplanted, inciting shouts of disapproval from the predominantly male crowd.

Riley: I don't know, I went to the bathroom and when I came back you were doing shots with the basketball team.

Blake: Why didn't you stop me?

Riley: I did. And after you put ten dollars in the jukebox and set it to play the same Taylor Swift song on repeat. We were basically asked to leave.

Blake: Thanks for driving me home.

Riley: Anytime.

Riley would never let anything bad happen to Blake. Not if he could help it. His pack always joked that he was all the chicks' favorite. He was because he was a fucking nice guy, a *good* guy, and he didn't see anything wrong with that. He grew up watching out for his mom. Being protective and sensitive was basically part of his DNA at this point. Even when he and Jasper were sharing, he was always the nice one. He was the one who made sure the girl was okay, was into it. He was the one who made sure she got home, checked on her the next day. Jasper never even remembered their damn names.

Jasper. The closer it got to Christmas break, the closer it got to Jasper moving to Greenly. Riley was increasingly nervous about introducing him to Blake. He'd want her, and he wouldn't understand why Riley hadn't already taken her. He'd want to share. Riley dragged his hands down his face, silently cursing the dilemma he knew was coming until his cell distracted him once again.

Blake: I'm ordering food. I want them to deliver it straight to my bed. You want in?

Riley: I have a paper to finish.

Riley had fallen a bit behind in his class load since he'd met Blake. It'd been easy enough to handle homework and training with his new team when those were the only things he did. Blake dragged him out of his room and out of his comfort zone on the daily. She liked to have fun, and she demanded he partake as well. She was a bit of a bad influence. More to the point, Jasper was going to be all over her.

Blake: So come do it here. My troll of a roommate is gone and as soon as I eat I'm going back to sleep. You'll have a full belly, peace and quiet, and the calming presence of your favorite person. What more could a reluctant baseball stud ask for?

Her words reminded him of a playful argument they'd gotten in last night before she'd hopped on the bar and started shaking her tight ass.

Riley: This baseball stud is still slightly pissed at how adamantly you agreed that basketball players were the true "gods of organized athletics."

Blake: Those gods were buying my drinks. I can't be held accountable for what I say out of gratitude. But, nonetheless, I apologize. Baseball rules, and basketball drools.

Riley threw his covers off, knowing that fighting her request was useless. He wasn't dumb. He knew he had free will and all that shit. However, it seemed the more time he spent with Blake, the more he wanted to make her happy. She was becoming part of his pack without even knowing it.

Concern tingled somewhere in the back of his brain, but he pushed it away. His family wasn't here, and he was inadvertently forming a bond with Blake. It made sense that she mattered to him, that her happiness mattered. He was a wolf, a shifter, he had instincts that demanded certain things of him. No big deal.

Riley: Be there soon.

Chapter Four

Riley made his way through campus, pulling his jacket around him to ward off the chill of the winter breeze. He wasn't usually bothered by the cold. He'd been in Colorado for most of his life, and was fine with the changeable weather. For some reason, the wind here in Greenly was cutting through to his bones. There were only five more days until Christmas break. Only five days until he would be home with his pack. He was planning on spending a few nights with Dom and Corey, and then heading to Jace and Axie's house.

They'd planned a big Christmas Eve dinner with the whole pack, everyone crashing there and waking up to open presents Christmas morning. He felt like a kid again. The idea of the holidays with his pack meant so much more since he'd been living away from them for so long.

He shivered, pulling his cell out of his pocket when it vibrated against his jean-clad thigh.

Blake: You left your laptop here.

Riley: I know, I'm walking over now to grab it.

Blake: We need to talk.

Riley rolled his eyes, already knowing where this conversation was headed.

Riley: Did you snoop through my computer?

Blake: Yes.

Riley: Is nothing sacred to you?

Blake: We met when I walked into your room unannounced to use your bathroom without permission.

He glanced up, making sure that he wasn't going to plow into a person or a bench while he was walking and texting at the same time. Campus was basically deserted today though, the windchill keeping everyone in their dorm rooms unless they absolutely had to leave for class.

Riley: I remember.

Blake: Anyway. You have a problem, and I really think you need to talk to someone about it.

Riley: You're so dramatic. It's not a problem, millions of people watch that stuff.

Blake: Look. There's a lot of things I can handle, but this? Good. Lord.

Riley: I'm not ashamed.

Blake: You own every season of the Real Housewives of Orange County. Every season. You OWN them Riley. Like you spent money so you could watch them more than once.

Riley: I like trashy reality TV. It's not a crime.

The truth was, re-watching those episodes made him feel better when he was missing Corey too much. He'd let them play in the background for three weeks after he'd moved into his dorm room. It'd made him feel a little less lonely. *Lonely.* He sighed, remembering how forlorn he'd felt until Blake had burst into his room. She'd filled his life with light, and he'd be forever grateful.

Blake: It should be.

Riley: Get out of my computer.

Blake: Your porn collection is also subpar.

Riley: Stop looking through my porn.

Only Blake would feel comfortable talking so casually about snooping through someone's private porn collection. His new bestie didn't have boundaries. She didn't even understand the word. Sometimes it was endearing and funny, sometimes it was invasive as fuck.

Blake: I'm going to upload some better-quality spank material for you, no worries.

Riley: Do NOT fill my computer with porn.

Blake: Too late. See you in a few.

Riley shoved his cell back into his pocket, resigned to the fact that his laptop would no doubt need to be tossed after it became filled to the brim with viruses. He had a hot-as-hell girl piling his computer with filthy porn, not really a reason to complain.

Although, every time she did something like this, something that reminded him of Jasper, he couldn't help but get a little twitchy.

Jasper was going to adore her, there was no doubt about it. Would that adoration turn into friendship like Riley's had? Or would it turn into a three-day fuck-fest, and then consequential awkwardness for the next four years?

Chapter Five

"Finallys are soon, right? That's what those big important tests are called? The ones you've been rambling about?"

Riley rolled his eyes at Jasper, making his friend smile on their FaceTime call. "My *finals* are over. I aced every single one of them, thanks for asking." Thankfully, Blake had begrudgingly agreed to him pausing the constant partying so he could get in a bit of studying. "And you better get the terminology down, you're joining me next semester."

"Yeah, yeah." He waved away his concern. "I'll get all the words right when I get there, don't worry, I won't embarrass you."

"We both know that's not true," Riley joked, making Jasper chuckle. "I can't wait to come home, bro, it's been weeks."

"I hate that you haven't had a chance to meet Allison yet." Allison was Jasper's cosmic little sister, like Hadley was Riley's. "She's so fucking cute."

"Yeah, me too, I can't wait to see her." Riley had been all packed and ready to head back to Haxton to meet Linc and Maddi's newborn daughter last month, but Jace had called and told him to stay at the dorms. Whichever mafia wannabe they'd been exposing at the time was acting like he was going to retaliate and they didn't want Riley vulnerable on the road to and from school. He assumed nothing more came of it since he hadn't gotten any more warnings from his pack.

"All right, I've got a meeting with Jace and Baze. I need to go be all serious and dull for a couple of hours."

Riley glanced at his watch, nodding. "Yeah, I've got lunch plans with Blake, I'll—"

"Blake *again*? You better not be replacing me, bro." He winked, letting Riley know he was joking.

"I could never replace you. You're one of a kind." He rolled his eyes again, his tone dripping with sarcasm. "Bye."

He clicked off the screen in the middle of Jasper's newest round of laughter. The truth was, Jasper *was* one of a kind, and he was completely irreplaceable. Also, Riley had never mentioned Blake was a girl. He knew Jasper would have so many questions, and he'd want pictures. He'd stalk her on social media and constantly ask Riley why he wasn't currently balls deep inside her. Then there would be comments about them sharing her when he moved to Greenly next semester. The torment would be endless, and Riley wasn't about to go down that road until he absolutely had to.

It'd been three weeks since Blake had come bouncing into his room all wrapped in pink. Three weeks of constant coffee breaks and study dates. They went to parties, they went to the movies, they had dinner, and played video games. In general, they hung out. Somehow, in the span of that time, she'd become his best friend. Which, she said, was her plan all along.

Blake was gorgeous, there was no denying it. Between her looks and her bubbly personality, she turned heads everywhere they went. But Riley had kept her at arm's length, had kept things between them platonic. Sure, she turned him on. When she'd dance with her tight little ass pressed up against his dick, he'd get hard as fuck. But he never acted on it.

He was a shifter, and shifters mated for life. He'd never seen the point in casual dating. It'd never made much sense to him. If the girl wasn't his forever, why even bother? He didn't want the hassle of a girlfriend if he knew that they'd only break up in the end.

That didn't mean he didn't hook up at parties. He did. *A lot.* Back in Haxton, he and Jasper had a bit of a notorious reputation. He was always down for a good time, and he was always down to share with his best friend. If it wasn't the girl he was going to spend the rest of his life with, what the hell did it matter? If they agreed to be passed back and forth, if they were into it, then no harm no foul.

When it came to Blake, he'd automatically put her in the best friend category. He didn't want to hurt her, and he didn't want to lead her on. He certainly didn't want sex to ruin their dynamic. He cared too much about her to fuck her, and he cared too much about her to date her. He'd never come right out and say it, but the fact that every guy in any given room was drooling at her feet and begging to take her home and he never had, must have clued her in.

"Hey, loser, let's go get some pizza." Blake came into his room, using the key she'd demanded when she realized he was the only person in the whole damn building that locked his door. "I'm starving."

He couldn't help but smile. She was dramatic, to say the least. Everything was to the extreme. If she was hungry, she was starving. If she was tired, she was utterly exhausted. If she was bored, she was contemplating joining the circus. Hell, the only reason he'd even met her was because she had to pee so bad, busting into a stranger's room seemed like an okay thing to do.

"Pizza it is then." He shut his laptop and got to his feet.

"Are you allowed to eat pizza?" Blake reached out and patted his stomach. "Spring training starts as soon as you get back from break. Don't you need to go on some kind of baller diet?"

Riley was a shifter, it wouldn't matter what he ate, he'd still have rippling abs and bulging arms. It was genetic, and he was more than blessed. He couldn't tell her that. He'd decided from the get-go to keep Blake as far away as possible from his other life: the supernatural one. The shifter world could be a dangerous one, as he'd learned over the last few years. Blake existed here at UNC, and that's where their friendship would stay.

"I don't diet, doll face." He tapped her chin, making her snort out a laugh. "But when I get back from Haxton, it's two-a-day extra batting practice, and better meals than burgers and pizza."

He worked out with his new teammates now, running and putting in time in the weight room. He always parted ways with them immediately afterward. He'd been so against making new friends, he'd been so bogged down in his own grief and sadness, he'd become antisocial. He wrapped it around him like a security blanket, like him missing his pack was the only way to keep them with him. Blake had lifted that weight off him.

"When the season starts, the girls are going to flock like flies." She sighed, like the thought alone was tiresome. "You're going to be impossible to deal with. I'm sure your ego is going to inflate and I'm going to have to knock you down every five minutes."

"Awe, doll face, don't be jealous." He slung his arm around her shoulder, pulling her in close. "You'll still be my number one, no matter how much ass I get after games."

She laughed, shoving him away playfully. "Just remember to wrap it before you tap it, stud. These girls would love nothing more than to hitch their future to a rising star."

He wrinkled his nose, the idea making him uncomfortable. "I always *wrap it*." He tapped the side of his head. "It's like rule number one, Barbie."

And it was. Shifter mating was a big deal, and the only female he'd ever bang without a condom would be the one he was destined to be with forever. Like, actually *forever*.

"You're going to have to stop calling me doll face and Barbie." She rolled her eyes, but reached for his hand, tugging him out the door and down the hall. "All your little admirers are going to think we're together, then their jealousy is going to spiral to a very dark place." She shrugged, dropping his hand and spinning to walk backward to face him. "And then the next thing you know, I've been replaced, my rabbit is going to be boiling in a pot on the stove and we'll all be a made-for-TV special about stalking, murder, and mayhem."

He threw his head back, chuckling loudly. "Number one: you are so fucking dramatic." He held up two fingers. "Number two: you don't even have a rabbit." When she opened her mouth to comment, he cut her off. "And no, I don't want to get into another discussion about your vibrators."

She giggled. "Okay, well, then is there a number three in there?" She spun back around, facing forward and pushing open the double glass doors that led to the front of the building.

"Number three." He put his hands on her shoulders, shaking her lightly. "You have big blue eyes and bouncing blonde curls, you look like a doll, and I call 'em like I see 'em."

"Yeah, yeah." She waved off his accurate description.

"Wait, there's a number four." He slung his arm back over her shoulders. "You, Blake 'Barbie Doll Face' Anderson, are one of my best friends. And *my* best friends? Are irreplaceable."

Chapter Six

Three days. Riley was actually counting them down on this little calendar he hid in his desk drawer. He was so excited to go home for a few weeks. He didn't care if that made him a pussy, and he didn't care if that made him a kiss-ass. He missed his pack; he missed his family. They were all still together, they couldn't possibly understand the way he felt.

He glanced over his shoulder when his door burst open, Blake bouncing in with her blonde curls and pretty blue eyes. "Sorry I'm late, I had to pack a bag. I'm bunking here tonight." She tossed her duffle on the floor by his closet and then jumped onto his bed. "My roommate's stupid boyfriend is staying in our room and if I had to spend another minute with them, my brain would explode into a million pieces."

He eyed her stuff, pursing his lips. "What if I had plans later?"

Blake threw her head back, propped up on her elbows and giggling her ass off. "Yeah right."

"I do stuff without you." Riley grabbed a pillow, hitting her lightly.

She held one finger. "You go to class." Then added a second. "And team training." She waggled her eyebrows, shimmying her shoulders. "Is that who your plans are with, stud? You got a date tonight with one of your teammates? If I were you, I'd go for that pitcher with the sideburns." She licked her lips like she wanted a taste of him as well.

He ignored her obvious interest in his teammate, because he was never jealous when it came to Blake and the guys she lusted after. "I could have a real date. It's possible."

She waved her hand in the air casually, then lay back on his pillows. "If you want to get your dick sucked tonight, walk down to the quad in your baseball jersey and I guarantee at least three girls will drop to their knees."

He snorted. "You aren't actually serious, are you? That doesn't happen in real life. Only in the porn you downloaded on my computer." Porn he'd watched, and thoroughly enjoyed.

Blake shrugged one shoulder. "I don't know. I'm sure there are girls here who would be more than happy to blow a hot baseball player in front of half the school."

He shook his head, knocking her with the pillow again. "You're so weird."

"I'm entertaining and delightful. There's a difference." She pushed her head into the pillows, kicked off her shoes and brought up her feet onto his bed. "Did you really have plans?" She wrinkled her nose like she might actually feel guilty for assuming he didn't.

Riley shook his head, closing his biology book. "No, I didn't have plans. I was going to get a jump on my reading for next semester and then start packing for winter break." He climbed on the bed with Blake, lying beside her with his shoulder touching hers. "When are you headed home?"

As excited and ready as he was to go back to Haxton and see his family, a small part of him knew he'd miss Blake while he was gone. He was so used to seeing her every day, her constant texts and laughter. His life was better with her in it, no doubt about that.

"I'm taking a bus, leaves tomorrow." She sighed, resting her head on his shoulder. "With all the snow headed our way, my dad is afraid my tires aren't up to the drive."

Riley liked that her father worried about her. It made him feel good to know that when she was home, she'd still have someone making sure she was safe. He put his cheek on the top of her blonde curls. "Why don't I drive you home? I can't leave 'til Friday, but it's not far out of my way, and I don't mind."

Blake sat up, smiling down at him. "Really? You sure you don't mind?"

"Nope. Don't mind at all."

"You're the best." She clapped her hands and peppered his cheeks with sloppy kisses. "I know I'd end up sitting next to some creeper on the bus who would fall in love with me and then subsequently stalk me until New Year's Eve."

He got off the bed, reaching under it to grab his giant duffle bag. "Were you born this dramatic? Or is it a skill you acquired over time?"

She pursed her lips, like she was seriously contemplating his question. "I'd say a little of both." She turned on her side. "I was born with a bit of a dramatic flair, but I've definitely honed it as I've aged."

Riley didn't doubt that at all. "You want to pick the food or the movie?" He moved to his closet and started pulling some things out to pack. They'd come up with a system over the last few weeks. Blake could either pick what they ate or what they watched. Riley couldn't do 90s action flicks *and* greasy cheeseburgers every time they had a sleep over.

"I want movie pick. It's almost Christmas, so a *Die Hard* marathon is very on point." She grabbed his remote control from his desk and got comfortable on his full-size bed. "I'll order though. Whatcha want, sourpuss?"

Riley didn't mind that the nickname stuck. "Grilled chicken and sala—"

Blake started making gagging noises before he could even finish his dinner order.

"You said it yourself. Spring training starts as soon as we get back. It's time I start eating like an athlete again, doll face." Blake didn't like healthy food, and getting her to eat anything green was a chore. "I pick dinner, those are the rules." He pointed to her cell where it was lying on the bed beside her. "Start dialing."

"You're the worst." She picked up her phone to place their order.

Riley rolled his eyes. "I'm the best when I'm offering to drive your ass home, but I'm the worst when I'm trying to get you to put something healthy in your body?" He threw one of his sweatshirts at her, knowing she'd ask for one to sleep in regardless of the overnight bag she packed. "Make up your mind."

"You're the best of the worst." She winked at him from under his covers as she slipped his shirt over her head. "Is broccoli still healthy if I smother it with cheese?"

"It's a start."

Chapter Seven

Riley was zipping up his duffle, more than ready to head back to Haxton for a few weeks. He couldn't wait to see Hadley, and he couldn't wait to meet Linc and Maddi's baby girl, Allison. But the thing he wanted to do the most? Run with his pack. He hadn't been able to shift since the last time he'd been home around Halloween and he was feeling a little twitchy.

Pen, Baze's mate, taught Shifter Culture at St. Leasing and she was always stressing how important it was for the guys to shift. To spend time in their wolf form. But here at UNC, Riley didn't know any other shifters. Didn't mean they didn't exist. It simply meant that there was no super-secret encrypted database showing him where all shifters went to college.

He tossed his bag across the room when it landed with a thud by his door. He was packed, he'd already filled his truck with gas, and now all he needed to do was load up the presents he'd bought for his family. Blake and he had gone shopping over the weekend, cramming the massive gifts search into one frantic afternoon. She'd insisted that it could be done, and she'd been right. He'd found presents for sixteen people in less than eight hours' time, Blake included. She'd picked hers out herself: a bubblegum pick cropped sweatshirt. It said *Nobody's Toy* across the chest. A nod to the fact he called her Barbie Doll.

His arms were piled high with perfectly wrapped gifts, complete with glittery bows, when his door burst open. "Hey, fucker."

Riley peered around the pile, shocked. "Jasper? What are you doing here?" He stepped backward, piling the presents on the top of his desk. "What... Is something wrong? Did something happen? One of the leaks, did they retaliate, is it—"

"Geez. Bro, calm the fuck down." Jasper chuckled, hugging Riley. "I figured since I was coming back to Greenly with you after the holidays, I'd leave my car here." He stepped back, shrugging before collapsing down onto the bed. "We can make the drive home together, and then in January, we won't be driving two cars back here."

"You drove two hours to drop off a car so you could get back in the car and drive another two hours with me?" Riley crossed his arms over his chest, eyes narrowed. "What gives, because I know you better than that."

Jasper grinned, stretching his arms up and behind his head. "I also figured we could push the trip home back a day." He sighed. "I've been on that compound for four months. I need to get some ass."

"There it is." Riley pulled the chair out from his desk, sitting down and facing his best friend. "All ready to plow through the single girls in Haxton?"

"And some not-so-single ones." Jasper smirked. "I figured one night on campus, a little play time with my best friend will tide us both over until the holidays with the pack are through."

Riley was beyond happy to see Jasper. He'd missed him the most. Well, second to Hadley of course. But Jasper's surprise visit meant he'd be meeting Blake a lot sooner than Riley had anticipated. He'd been worried what their relationship would look like, and now, it seemed, he was about to find out.

"I'm giving Blake a ride home too. We can't push the trip off another night." Riley didn't want to push the trip off. He didn't want the two of them getting drunk together. He knew their personalities, and he knew the chaos that would ensue. It'd be like a match meeting a crate of dynamite.

"Okay, no big deal. At least I'll get to meet him on the ride back." Jasper clapped his hands together. "I finally get to meet the man who has replaced me."

Oh, and about that. Riley had yet to tell Jasper Blake was a girl and not some dude he'd been palling around with over the last few weeks. He sighed, pulling out his cell and texting his new best friend to inform her his OG best friend was in town.

Riley: Hey, you packed?

Blake: Yeah, you ready to hit the road? I got road trip food and I even made us a playlist. Super dope of me right?

He glanced at the stack of gifts on his desk, then to Jasper, who was scrolling through his phone on Riley's bed. He wished he was ready to hit the road.

Riley: Do people still say dope?

Blake: Thinking of bringing it back. You want me to come to you or you picking me up?

Riley: Actually, I have a last-minute surprise for you.

Blake: Ooooo is it a puppy?

No. It was two fucking wolves. The irony made him chuckle to himself. "Is this guy funnier than me? I'm trying not to be jealous, dude, but damn." Jasper's narrowed gaze was on Riley's phone, like he could see through the back of it to find what made Riley laugh.

Riley: Jasper surprised me, he came to drop his car off and make the drive home with me. He didn't know I was giving you a ride.

Blake: I get to meet the infamous Jasper? Wow. A puppy would have been better, but this is a close second.

Riley: One more thing…

Blake: And you call me dramatic? What's with the ominous?

Riley smiled at her text, calling him out for his loaded pause. Her dramatics were rubbing off on him. That was the only explanation.

Riley: Jasper thinks you're a dude.

Blake: Uh, should I be offended?

Riley: He assumed and I never corrected him.

Blake: Why? Is he a sexist douche who wouldn't accept a chick as your best friend?

Riley: No. He's a horny douche who would've wanted to meet and bang you immediately.

His eyes cut to Jasper, who was still playing on his phone.

Blake: I'm bang-able. It's a blessing and a curse. But I can assure you the last thing I want to do is mess up my friendship with you. You're my favorite, sourpuss.

Riley: He's going to hit on you the whole ride home. Let me apologize in advance.

Jasper wouldn't be able to help himself where Blake was concerned. She was gorgeous and witty. She could dish it out as good, if not better than she could take it. Jasper had already admitted he was in the middle of a dry spell back in Haxton. Which meant he'd be hornier than usual.

Blake: I can handle him, no worries. You going to tell him I'm dickless? Or just let me show up and shock the shit out of him?

Riley: Leaning toward shock.

Blake: Again. You call me dramatic?

Riley: I'm picking up your bad habits.

Blake: Whatever you say, sourpuss. I'll be there soon.

Chapter Eight

Jasper was still relaxing on Riley's bed, his eyes assessing the dorm room. Riley knew what he was seeing, knew his room was bare and void of any personality. This place wasn't home. Until Riley met Blake, he'd hated being in Greenly without his best friend. The only thing he'd added to the space when he'd moved in was his own bedding and the framed picture of his pack. There was a picture of him and Blake taped to the bathroom mirror of them at a party, her on his back laughing. She'd printed it and told Riley the bathroom was where it belonged since his toilet was the reason they'd met in the first place.

"I'm assuming Jace is having the guy next door booted out so we can be neighbors next semester?" Jasper sat up. "Guess it pays to have a tech-savvy evil genius as a twin." He placed his booted feet to the floor. "Next year we're moving off campus though."

Another reason Riley hadn't made an effort to meet his neighbors. He knew Jace would have whoever lived next door now moved down the hall so he and Jasper could live next to each other. Riley was happy to get a house with Jasper next year. He was sure Jace would help them qualify to buy the place since the pack beta didn't believe in *renting*. He said it was flushing money down a proverbial drain.

"Sounds good to me, bro."

Maybe they could find something on the edge of town, close to the woods. That way they could shift and run whenever they had the urge. Riley hadn't really given much thought to his wolf while he'd been at UNC without any of his brothers. Now that Jasper was here, he felt an itch in his skin, like it was too tight for his body. He suddenly couldn't wait to get home and let his wolf out to play.

"Your boy Blake could move in too, granted I think he's cool as you make him sound." Jasper was jealous of Blake, even if he joked about it. Riley knew his friend well enough to sense those undertones, supernatural abilities aside. Jasper was pissy about being replaced, even though staying in Haxton for the fall semester to help Jace and Axie had been his idea. Jasper had FOMO, in any and every situation. If he'd have come to Greenly when Riley had, he would have wanted to be home with his twin fighting the evil men of the shifter underworld. "Speaking of your new bro crush, where is he?" He glanced down at his watch, like making them wait was a point against Blake.

Riley was abnormally quiet, his stomach in knots about his worlds colliding. He kept pacing the room while worst-case scenarios went through his head. By worst case, he meant Jasper and Blake immediately fucking on his full-size bed. He knew it was irrational, but that was where he was mentally. "Blake will be here." She was always late. She probably walked out of her building and realized she'd forgotten her phone, or decided she was *in dire need of caffeine* on the walk over and decided to stop for coffees.

"Why do you seem so nervous? You're giving off some odd-as-fuck vibes." Jasper's eyes narrowed, his hands going to his hips. "Did you flip your coin? Are you actually into this guy? I mean, I know you're okay swinging your dick in front of me but—"

"Stop." Riley rolled his eyes at Jasper's ridiculous question. He wasn't gay any more than Jasper was. They shared because it was what they'd always done. It started by accident, and they'd quickly realized neither of them had a problem with it. In fact, they got a kick out of it. They never bothered to get serious with any chick, they were shifters, what was the point? But him being comfortable like that with Jasper didn't mean he'd ever allow it to happen with anyone else. Jasper was his pack, his family. "You know that's not what's up."

"No?" Jasper's eyebrow raised. "Because you're on edge, and twitchy, like you're afraid for me to meet this guy."

He wasn't wrong on that front. Riley was terrified Jasper would end up ruining his friendship with Blake—something Riley didn't ever want to see happen. She'd saved him, she'd brought him out of his shell and demanded he start living like a college freshman. He owed her, and he liked her. He knew he'd miss the shit out of her if Jasper drove a wedge between them, and more than anything else, he didn't want any animosity between him and his packmate.

Before Riley could shoot off a response, his door flew open dramatically, banging the wall behind it. "Sorry it took me so long, but I forgot my phone, and I brought coffees." Blake came into the room like she owned it, which was how she entered most rooms, welcome or not. She was wearing tight jeans with a cropped sweater, her blonde curls bouncing on top of her head as she balanced a drink carrier with three large to-go cups.

Riley's gaze flew to Jasper, wanting to see his immediate reaction. Jasper's jaw dropped, his eyes wide. He was surprised, to say the least.

Blake stepped over to him, handing him a coffee and reaching out to close his mouth with the tip of her finger under his chin. "I know, I know. Riley let you think I had a big ol' dick." She giggled, passing a coffee to Riley as well. "As you can see, I don't."

Jasper glanced down to Blake's crotch, then looked at Riley. "Blake is a chick."

"Yep." He took a sip of his coffee, hoisting the gifts off his desk with one hand.

Jasper held his hand out, shaking Blake's. "It's nice to meet you, no-dick Blake."

She laughed again, dropping his hand to swing her duffle off the ground where she'd dropped it. "It's nice to meet you too." She cut her eyes to Riley. "I don't know why this one never corrected you but—"

"I do." Jasper reached out, taking Blake's bag off her shoulder and transferring it to his own like the gentlemen he *wasn't*, while he glared at Riley. "He didn't want me to give him shit about whether you two were fucking. Plus, I'd have cyberstalked the hell out of you."

Which hadn't altogether worked because Jasper had accused him of hooking up with Blake *with* a dick. "Tell me you wouldn't have constantly asked me if I was hitting it with her?" Riley held his door open for everyone to file out, wanting to get Blake home and away from Jasper. "You have a one-track mind, bro."

"True that." Jasper was walking backward, his eyes appreciatively assessing Blake. "And are you?"

"No, he's not." She hooked her arm through Riley's, resting her head on him affectionately. "And neither one of us want to hear shit about it." She fluttered her lashes at Jasper. "He's the best thing that ever happened to me, no sex required."

Riley kissed the top of her head, happy to see that she was cutting off Jasper's bullshit at the knees. Predictably, he could also see Jasper's reaction to and appreciation of Blake's body in his packmate's gaze. Gorgeous, sassy, outspoken. Like he'd thought, Blake was catnip to Jasper, who held his hands out, placatingly. "All right, I hear you. No questions about why the hell the two of you aren't nailing on the daily." He mimed locking his lips and throwing away the key.

Riley knew Jasper would keep his mouth shut *until* the moment after they dropped Blake at her front door. Then he'd be on him. He'd demand to know what the hell was going on, and he'd give him crap for keeping him in the dark to begin with. They had over an hour's drive ahead of them. Riley would enjoy the peace while he could.

Blake wasn't falling all over Jasper's good looks, and she certainly wasn't flirting. She'd shown her loyalty to Riley instantly. And, for the most part, Jasper was behaving.

Thinking back on it, Riley wasn't sure why he'd made Blake's gender a secret from his best friend. It seemed almost silly to be so possessive about his platonic relationship with Blake. Jasper was always going to find out, always going to meet her at some point. Riley wasn't a selfish person, other than about Corey when she was pregnant with his cosmic sister. That was straight shifter nature there though, and his relationship with Blake had zero to do with his shifter.

Chapter Nine

Jasper was telling Blake embarrassing stories about Riley, stemming all the way back to their freshman year at St. Leasing. She was cracking up, begging for more as soon as he'd finished one humiliating story. Riley wanted to be irritated, but the fact that Jasper wasn't outwardly flirting with her was helping. He'd been so worried, and it seemed it was for nothing. Blake and Jasper were getting along, but there was no sexual tension in the air. Riley's senses would have picked up on it. His wolf wouldn't be able to miss it.

It started to snow as soon as they pulled out the campus gates, and now it was really coming down. The flakes were large white blurs, and Riley needed to use the windshield wipers to clear them away. The sun was rapidly setting, and he was wishing he'd have checked the weather before getting on the road.

"Riley is everyone's favorite back home. He dotes on all the females, and rocks all the babies. Peacekeeper and such an ass-kisser." Jasper chuckled, using the term loudly while he could. If Dom or any of the other coaches heard Jasper refer to Riley's relationship with their mates that way, they'd pop him for sure.

"No, he's such a *sweetheart.*" Blake rubbed his shoulders from her spot behind him in the backseat. "The best friend a girl could ever ask for."

"Sweetheart?" Jasper pursed his lips, his gaze meeting Riley's briefly. "Maybe to you, and the women in our family, but make no mistake, I've seen this guy be a class A douchebag."

Riley rolled his eyes. They both knew that wasn't true. He was always kind to the chicks he and Jasper were with. He never made promises he couldn't keep, never wanted anyone to get hurt. "Douchebag? No way, man. That's you, and you damn well know it."

"Well, someone has to be the bad cop with the girls." Jasper winked at Blake, his oblique reference to their sharing making her smile grow wide and curious. "Otherwise, we'd never get rid of them. They'd become addicted AF." Riley saw her reaction in the rearview mirror, and he stifled a groan.

"Wait a minute, good cop? You guys are into role play or something kinky like that?" Blake's gaze was darting between them, her smile never faltering.

Jasper turned in his seat, mock indignation on his face. "Are you telling me Riley has been keeping secrets from you too?" He tsked at his packmate. "Bro, friends don't keep—"

"Don't, man, don't go there." Riley spoke softly, but put some force behind his words. Blake didn't need to know anything about his sex life, or Jasper's. She'd never be part of it, and Riley wasn't about to share with her. "There's no reason."

Blake gasped, slapping both his seat and Jasper's. "Well now I *have* to know. I'll *die* from curiosity. You know I will." Her tone was pleading in the extreme, and adorably dramatic. "Please, Riley."

"No."

Jasper's cell blasted out a ring before Riley could shut her demands down any further.

"It's Jace." Jasper answered by the third ring, the lollipop Blake had given him from her purse still sticking out the side of his mouth. "Hey, man, what's up." There was a short pause. "Yeah, no shit, we're driving in it." Another pause. "Oh fuck, really?" Pause. "Send me the address." He paused, his head nodding. "Yeah, I hear you. We'll be safe." He sighed. "Bye."

"What was that about?" Riley glanced in the rearview mirror, checking Blake's reaction to the one-sided conversation. "Everything okay at home?" Jasper had to get what Riley was carefully trying to ask, not wanting to alert Blake to anything she shouldn't know. Like shifters were real, and Jace was fighting cruel underworld bosses at every turn.

"Yeah, man, everything is good at home." Jasper leaned forward, peering into the now-dark night, trying to see through the large snowflakes like Riley had been trying to do for the last fifteen minutes. "Jace said the blizzard has closed a few roads ahead of us. We can't get to Blake's tonight, and we can't get much farther. Forward or back. The roads are a fucking mess, man," Jasper said. "Campus is getting hit hard too."

Riley already knew he messed up by not checking the weather report before they left campus. "What address is Jace sending you? Did he find a motel close by or something?" Riley was already dreading the night ahead of them. How was he supposed to keep Blake's curiosity at bay and Jasper's mouth shut tight when they were all locked together with nothing else to do but watch cable or the snow continuing to fall?

"How did Jace know where we were? Or that roads were closed? Is this guy tracking your phones?" Blake glanced to Riley, then back to Jasper. "Are you secretly in the CIA? Good cop, bad cop?"

Jasper chuckled, turning around to tug on one of her blonde curls. "Nah, Jace is an extreme tech-y. He tracks everyone's phones when we're on the road, which turned out to be a good thing because he has a safe house just—"

"A safe house? Why does a tech-y nineteen-year-old need a safe house?"

Jasper's gaze quickly met Riley's, a wince on his face. "Jace is a bit of a doomsday prepper with too much money." Riley shrugged like it was no big deal, going for casual to explain away his friend's twin not only tracking them but sending them to a safe house. "He has houses everywhere and he plays with technology like Jasper plays with his dick."

"Hey, don't act like you don't—"

"What's the address?" Riley cut him off, grinning at his indignant expression.

Jasper leaned forward and entered the address into the truck's navigation system. "It's only a few miles away. He said it's a little cabin in the middle of nowhere, but the truck should be able to make it there, no problem."

Blake pursed her lips. "Are you taking me to a creepy cabin in the woods so you can murder me and bury my body?"

"No." Riley expected nothing less from Blake. She was always dramatic and sarcastic. He also knew how weird the last-minute detour sounded. "Zero plans to murder you. Tonight." He winked at her in the rearview mirror.

Jasper turned in his seat again, his tone playful. "Do you have any idea how lucky you are? I mean, a night in a secluded cabin with us. You just won the lottery, girl."

Blake threw her head back, laughing loudly. "Oh yeah?"

"I have references. Would you like to speak to them?" Jasper pulled his cell back out of his pocket and Riley knocked it down to the floorboard before he could dial up any of their conquests.

Chapter Ten

The cabin was small, but clean. There was almost a foot of snow gathering on the side of the small gravel road leading to it. He'd put the truck in four-wheel drive to get them there safely. The cabin's front door had an electronic lock, and Jasper entered the code then opened the door, letting Blake go inside first. The place smelled like cedar and old smoke. There was a long couch in the middle of the room, a large fireplace with stacks of wood on either side, and that was about it. It was one room, and the kitchen cabinets were empty except for one lone bottle of whiskey and a can of chicken noodle soup. As far as safe houses went, this one was a pretty bare setup, especially for Jace Franklin.

"Good thing I brought road trip snacks." Blake closed the empty fridge and pulled a giant bag of cheddar popcorn out of her tote. "But the whiskey works." She grabbed it off the counter and tossed it across the room to Jasper.

His packmate caught it easily and opened the cap, the sound of the plastic giving way filling the silence in the dark room. Jasper took a swig, then passed it to Riley. "I'll start the fire, but we're going to need to pull some warm clothes out of our suitcases since I don't see any blankets."

Blake took the bottle from Riley, eyeing the one lone sofa. "The three of us sharing that bad boy?"

Jasper glanced at her over his shoulder, winking. "Don't worry, Barbie. We've got a system down."

"Do I have Mattel stamped on my ass?" Blake spun in a circle like a puppy chasing her tail. "Or do the two of you share one brain? Doll Face, Barbie. I'm dyeing my hair."

Riley sighed deeply, taking the whiskey back from Blake. "Enough, Jasper." He took another long swig then bent down to open his suitcase, pulling a large sweatshirt out and handing it to Blake. Then a sweater for Jasper and another pullover for himself. Since the one-room cabin was small, once they got the fire going, they should all stay plenty warm. "Blake, you can take the couch, Jasper and I will be fine on the floor."

Jasper stepped back when the fire caught with a whoosh and warm light filled the room. He peered down at the floor, a frown on his face. "I'm not sleeping on this floor." He shook his head. "There aren't even any pillows, bro."

"Don't be a spoiled brat." Riley threw a pair of sweatpants at his packmate harder than necessary. "You can make your own pillow."

"Riley, it's fine." Blake sank down onto the couch. "We share a bed all the time, and I'm sure we can make room for Jasper. No one needs to sleep on the hard cold floor."

Jasper's eyes widened. "Besties who share a bed but don't fuck in it? Seems suspish."

"Give it a rest, man. I thought you said you'd keep your mouth shut." Riley could feel a headache coming on quick. He'd been prepared to spend two hours in the car with Jasper and Blake, but not an overnight in a secluded cabin with no Wi-Fi. Jasper was going to get bored, and the more bored he got, the more he was going to run his mouth. He was like a toddler, constantly needing entertaining.

Jasper got behind the couch, pushing it closer to the fire with Blake still on it. He sat on one side of her and reached across her lap, patting the other side for Riley. "Come on, I'll be good. Scouts' honor."

Riley joined them, kicking his long legs up to rest his feet on the fireplace hearth. He put his arm along the back of the couch and Blake settled into his side. It was natural, it was normal, the connection the two of them had formed almost from the start. Now though, there were three, and they stayed silent for a few minutes, watching the flames and passing around the now half-empty bottle of whiskey. Riley was happy to be with two of his favorite people; he adored Blake and he'd missed his packmate. So he laid his head back, letting himself absorb the moment as the whiskey warmed him from the inside out.

"I'm bored." Jasper clapped his hands, putting an abrupt end to Riley's peaceful moment.

"Same." Blake bounced in her seat, her curls moving with her.

Great, now he was surrounded by toddlers who needed constant stimulation to stay out of trouble. Riley swore if he turned his back, one of them would be climbing the walls while the other set fire to the couch.

"Truth or dare." Riley outwardly groaned at Jasper's suggestion. Truth or dare wouldn't lead anywhere good, that was for fucking sure.

Riley shook his head, removing his arm from around Blake. "No way."

"There are no cards, no board games. We've got hours until any of us are going to feel tired enough for sleep thanks to Blake's evening coffee run. So. All in favor of truth or dare, raise your hand." Jasper put his hand in the air, smiling wide when Blake did the same.

Riley glared at both of them, making Blake giggle. "Oh, come on, sourpuss. Jasper is right. There isn't really anything else to do." Blake got on her knees, her hands on Riley's shoulders, shaking him playfully. "Let's play. It'll be fun."

Riley knew truth or dare with Jasper and Blake would be a lot of things, but fun was not one of them. Nope. It was a disaster waiting to happen. Jasper would get horny, Blake would get curious, and Riley would grow more irritated with the whole situation until it combusted. This, this right here was why Riley had longed to keep his two worlds separate. Part of him knew the moment they came together it would be a crash that shook him to the core.

"I'll start." Jasper stood, backlit from the roaring fire. "Riley, truth or dare?"

Riley sighed. He'd be damned no matter which option he chose. Neither Jasper nor Blake accepted the word *no* all that well. "Dare."

Jasper tapped his chin, his eyes narrowed, like he was trying to come up with something good. "Go piss your initials into the snow."

Riley snorted, getting to his feet. "Really? Done." He was pleasantly surprised by Jasper's easy juvenile dare. He was sure his best friend was going to say something completely sexual having to do with Blake. Riley undid his pants on his way to the front door, standing on the lowest porch step and pissed three letters into the snow. He didn't do a bad job, but uppercase R's were hard. He headed back inside. "Done." He zipped his jeans and plopped back down on the couch. "My turn. Jasper, truth or dare?"

"Dare." Jasper crossed his arms over his chest.

"Go eat the yellow snow."

Blake laughed and Jasper's jaw dropped open. "Dude, I am not eating your piss snow. What's the penalty for not following through on a dare?"

Blake held up the whiskey bottle, shaking it. "Do a shot."

Jasper grabbed the bottle from her, tipping it back and downing more than a shot. He wiped his mouth with the back of his hand. "Blake, truth or dare?"

"Truth. I'm not about to try to piss my initials in the snow." Blake was still sitting on her knees, her body pressed close to Riley's. He took off his second pullover, the heat from the fire and the warmth from Blake's body making him feel a little flushed. The whiskey probably wasn't helping either.

"Tell us the kinkiest thing you've ever done." Jasper's gaze cut to Riley's. He knew why his packmate had asked her that. He knew what Jasper was trying to judge for himself. Riley's jaw clenched, his muscles tightening to the point of pain. This wasn't the first time he'd heard Jasper ask a girl that question, and it was always leading. Jasper hadn't lied when he cryptically told Blake they had a system.

"I knew you'd go to sex. So predictable." Blake rolled her eyes. "Uh, let's see. The kinkiest? I hooked up with a basketball player this year under the full bleachers while he was supposed to be in the locker room for halftime."

Jasper nodded, a smirk on his face. "Public sex. Not bad."

"My turn." Blake grinned, basically vibrating in her seat. "Riley, truth or dare?" He opened his mouth to say dare but she interrupted him. "Truth? Okay, great. What has Jasper been not-so-subtly running his whore mouth about? System? Good cop, bad cop? I've gotta know."

Riley closed his eyes, dropping his head forward in irritation. Even when Jasper promised to keep his trap shut, he opened it and let shit fall out. "I take the penalty." He took the whiskey from her hands as she pouted, taking a healthy swig. "Jasper, truth or dare?

Dare? Perfect, I dare you to keep your fucking mouth closed, like you promised, until we drop Blake off at home tomorrow."

Jasper chuckled, taking the whiskey bottle from him. "I'll take the penalty." He tsked, his eyes dancing with wicked humor. "You really shouldn't be so ashamed of who you are, bro."

Riley gave a slight shake of his head, warning his packmate not to cross him. He wasn't ashamed of antics with Jasper, he never had been. Not once. That didn't mean that he wanted Blake involved. He'd vowed to keep her separate from the supernatural side of his existence, and that included his extracurricular activities with his best friend.

"You know I'm going to keep asking until someone tells me, right? You can't throw out vague shit like that and not expect me to get curious." She turned to Jasper, her head cocked to the side. "That was your plan all along, right? You wanted me to ask. You're so predictable."

"Seems my man here has developed a nasty habit of keeping secrets from the people he loves." Jasper sat on the hearth, facing Blake and Riley. "Too many secrets will eat you alive, bro. I'm simply trying to keep you breathing."

Riley and Jasper both were well versed in secrets. They kept their shifter nature secret for their whole lives. They kept secrets about the men Jace and Axie were taking out one by one. They dealt with and lived in secrets. Jasper wanted Blake to ask. He wanted Blake to know because he wanted her to be intrigued. He *wanted* to share her, had since the first moment she'd bounced into Riley's dorm room and he realized who she was.

Riley saw that now, and it pissed him the fuck off. Jasper got bored easier than a kid in church, and the minute they'd entered the cabin he'd made his mind up. What better way to spend a night than sharing Blake in front of the fire? What better way to get back at Riley for keeping Blake's identity from him? Jasper wanted to get his dick wet. He wanted to have Blake, and he wanted to punish Riley.

The detour to the empty, secluded cabin had given him the perfect opportunity to hit a whole flock of birds with one stone.

Chapter Eleven

Riley ground his molars together, his body tense. He couldn't remember the last time he'd been this angry with Jasper. He didn't know if there was a time when he'd wanted to kick his packmate's ass this badly. He couldn't do that though, not in front of Blake. Two shifters fighting, even in human form, was too risky. It would be too violent, too rough. She'd be scared, and she'd have even more questions. It was too late to keep Blake separate from Jasper, but he could still save her from learning about his wolf. Knowing about his pack, becoming too intertwined with them, would be dangerous for her. Look at what happened to Corey, Madden, Pen...even Axie. Their supernatural side of the world wasn't always bonded mates and happy babies.

"While you two have this little pissing contest, I'm going to run to the restroom." Blake hopped up. "After that, I want to hear the real story behind Jasper's thinly veiled attempts to lure me in. Annoyingly, it worked."

Jasper waited until they heard the bathroom door click close. "Come on, man, what's the big deal?" He put his hands behind his head, resting back like he didn't have a care in the world. "It's not like you two are hooking up."

"And it's not like you two *ever* will." Riley sat up, training his narrowed eyes on his packmate. "You hear me?"

Jasper held his hand up. "I don't want your girl."

Riley shook his head, not even needing to speak out loud for Jasper to understand what he meant. Blake wasn't his girl, but he'd be damned if she got involved with Jasper either.

Riley had spent a lot of time with her over the last few weeks. If she was meant to be his forever, then he would've known it by now. Same with Jasper. If she was meant for his best friend, he would've felt it.

Blake was human, and she wasn't supposed to be part of their world. Riley would do everything he could to keep her out of it, keep her from getting hurt. There was no future for her with him or Jasper, other than friendship. Sex with two shifters? It wasn't normal, it was altogether *more*. It tended to become an addiction for the girls they were with. Jasper was a horny bastard, but he wasn't cruel. If Riley couldn't get Jasper's dick to listen, maybe he could appeal to his heart.

"We'll ruin her, and you know it. She's my friend. Why would you want to put her through that?"

Jasper rolled his eyes. "We've been with plenty of girls, and they're fine."

"They're fine *now*, but they weren't fine right after. They know. They know what we did together wasn't normal. They know we're different." Riley hadn't been lying when he said he was the nice one, that he made sure all the girls were okay. It took time. It took Riley turning them down over and over again. He dodged questions, he made excuses. He covered their tracks, always. "Blake is my friend. I don't want to have to ice her out of our lives. I don't want to push her away for her own good."

"She seems like a big girl to me, bro. Not one who lowers herself to chase dick once it walks out of the room."

Riley got to his feet, stepping closer to Jasper and lowering his voice. "This. *This* is why I never told you about her. I knew you'd end up pulling some bullshit."

"We'll drop her at home tomorrow. She'll have all of winter break to forget about it. By the time we see her back on campus, everything will be fine." Jasper smirked. "Unless there's another reason you don't want me to touch her?"

"She's not for me." Riley grabbed the whiskey bottle back from Jasper, taking another long swig. "But if you fuck up my friendship with her, I'll never forgive you." Jasper was still wearing that stupid smirk so Riley added, "And I'll tell Madden what you did."

That wiped the shit-eating grin off his face. Jasper had a relationship with Madden like Riley had with Corey. Disappointing someone who was a cross between your sister and your surrogate mother? Not a good feeling.

"Okay, losers." Blake sauntered into the room and sank back down on the couch, eyeing the two of them with a wicked smile on her pretty face. "Tell me what's going on. You two look like you're seconds away from ripping out each other's throats. It's hot, but I don't want to spend my night cleaning up blood."

"Riley doesn't want you to hear any stories." Jasper shrugged, like he hadn't thrown Riley under the bus.

"Oh." Blake pouted, her gaze turning to Riley. "Would it help if I shared more stories about myself? I don't mind sharing. Let's see, there was this one time at a party where my ex showed up and we ended up in a shed in the backyard and—"

"Stop." Riley covered his ears. "I don't want to hear a blow-by-blow of your sexual history." He sighed, completely over this whole day.

"Oh." Blake tugged her bottom lip between her teeth. "I would never judge you. You know that right? You're my best friend. I just want to know you. I want to know who you are when you're with your family. That's all."

Fucking fantastic. Now his attempt to keep her safe was hurting her feelings. Riley sighed and dropped his head to his chest. He would beat the shit out of Jasper once they got back to Haxton, no doubt about it. As soon as they pulled into the driveway at Corey and Dom's place, he would knock his bitch ass out cold. Then he'd leave him on the front lawn to sleep it off in the snow.

Riley cut his gaze to Jasper, letting him see the anger hiding behind the calm. The minute the three of them stepped foot inside this one-room cabin, their night was laid out for them. Jasper and Blake were too similar, they got bored in the same ways. He knew both of them as well as he knew himself. It was inevitable. It was what he'd been trying to avoid. What he'd wanted to keep from happening. It was always going to go this way though, wasn't it? If not tonight, then another night on campus after a crazy party. A spring break trip gone wrong. Late-night studying fueled by Adderall and coffee. Unless he wanted to give Blake up completely, the three of them were inevitable.

"Jasper and I share girls, we always have. I honestly don't remember a time when I was with someone without him there. The first girl we slept with was older than us. A senior at the public school our freshman year at St. Leasing. We met at a party and she wanted us both. It was fun, we liked it, so we kept doing it."

Blake's eyebrows raised to her hairline. "You *only* share?"

Jasper shrugged. "Mostly. Not only."

"But you two don't hook up?"

"No." Riley shook his head. "It's not like that."

"How can it not be?" Blake wagged her finger between the two shifters flanking her. "There are a lot of moving parts when you're sharing. How do things not get, uh, crossed?"

"We're pros by this point." Jasper took another sip from the whiskey bottle, then passed it over to Blake. "Riley is good cop, because he's a good guy. I'm bad cop because I'm an asshole." Riley watched as Jasper eyed Blake, looking her up and down. "So? What do you say? Wanna play?"

Blake choked on the whiskey she'd just sipped. "Excuse me?"

"We both know why you wanted to know the story. If you weren't interested, you'd have ignored my bullshit and let it go the first time Riley asked you to. You're curious as fuck and there's nothing else to do here." Jasper stood, pulling his shirt over his head and tossing it to the dirty ground he refused to sleep on. "You call the shots here, gorgeous, just give us the word."

Riley's hands were fisted at his sides, his heart beating wildly in his chest. He was so fucking torn. He wanted to kill his best friend, he wanted to hit him until he was unconscious. He wanted to grab him by the hair and drag him out of the cabin, he wanted to throw him into the snow and watch as he slowly froze to death.

But.

He also wanted Blake to say yes. Suddenly, he wanted to know what she sounded like while she came apart between them. Riley hated himself in that moment, hated the lust that was starting to run through his veins. He hated that his wolf was awake now, when he'd been all but dormant for the whole damn semester.

Blake's eyes met his, her perpetual smile dimming. "This what you want too?"

"He wants it as much as he doesn't want it." Jasper jerked his head in Riley's direction. "He's afraid this will change things between you two. He's afraid that it'll ruin everything. He's turned on though. He's into it."

Riley detested how well his packmate knew him. How well he could interpret his warring emotions. Jasper's wolf was always closer to the surface, especially when it came to his reaction to females. Which meant Jasper could sense Riley's mood the moment it shifted toward lust and away from annoyance. Jasper simplified things that were more complicated than the bottom line. Riley wouldn't touch Blake, not if it meant he'd lose her. This, what was about to happen between the three of them, was never his plan. Never.

"Will you hate me afterward?" Blake was only looking at Riley, her tone vulnerable for probably the first time since they'd met.

Riley shook his head, answering honestly. "I could never hate you, doll face."

"As much as it pains me to admit it, Jasper's right, I'm curious." Blake still wasn't looking anywhere but at him. "I won't do this if you don't want to go through with it. I don't want him without you."

That helped clarify things, as odd as it sounded. Knowing if he said no, the whole thing would drop. Blake was breathing heavy, her face flushed. It was the whiskey, the warmth from the fire, but it was also the anticipation. She wanted to do this, she wanted to be shared.

He couldn't blame her. Most girls were curious. Most women wanted to experience it, even if only once. It was taboo, it was forbidden. Yet here was her best friend and his best friend. Which made Jasper safe. They were offering her a harmless space to explore. Blake grabbed life by the horns, was always down to try something new. Riley had known she would be catnip to Jasper, but what he hadn't counted on was Jasper offering something Blake would find so enticing.

If he said no, this thing would still be between them. It already existed. The sexual tension was thick, and the words couldn't be unsaid. Jasper had ruined his relationship with Blake.

Riley wanted to rage. He wanted to weep. He also wanted to make Blake sit on his face.

Fucking Jasper.

Riley sighed, studying her gorgeous blue eyes. "This really what you want?" Blake started to smile, nodding. "This is a one-time deal, you understand?" She nodded again. "We do this together, and it never leaves this cabin. Nothing changes when we all get back to campus."

"Nothing changes. Gotta try everything once though, right?" Blake rose up on her knees, her bottom lip between her teeth again. "After tonight, I'll forget it ever happened. Promise."

Jasper had been silent while he waited for Riley to make up his mind, but he scoffed at her words. He knew as well as Riley, Blake would never forget tonight. She'd never forget the way it felt for them to share her.

They weren't human.

And even if her brain didn't know that, her body would.

Chapter Twelve

Jasper's shirt was already on the floor, and when Riley didn't protest anymore, Jasper unbuckled his belt and let his jeans fall to the ground as well. He was standing in front of the fire in his boxer briefs, his eyes alight with mischief and excitement. Riley's jaw clenched. His whole body wired like the string of a hunter's bow. This wasn't what he'd planned, it wasn't what he would've chosen for Blake. He'd wanted them to be friends. Only friends. Now that it was right in front of him, ripe for the picking, he was having a hard time not mirroring Jasper's mood.

Riley pulled off his Henley, letting it join the growing pile at their feet. He knew his chest was heaving, and his racing heart had his pulse pounding in his neck. He knew Jasper could tell, his quiet chuckle giving him away.

Riley watched as his packmate stepped forward, taking Blake's hand and helping her to her feet. "This is what you want, doll, right?" He waited for her to nod and then his fingers clasped the hem of Riley's sweatshirt, dragging it up and off her petite body. "Then let's get the show on the road, yeah?"

"The show?" Blake snorted out a laugh, taking the liberty to remove her t-shirt, leaving her standing before them in tight jeans and a soft pink lacy bra. Her breasts spilled out of the cups so temptingly Riley licked his lips.

Jasper missed nothing, laughing quietly at his reaction. "I think our boy likes what he sees." He put his hands on Blake's hips, placing small kisses down the column of her neck while his fingers worked the button on her pants. "You just gonna watch tonight, bro? Not usually your style."

Riley had never been content to be a bystander, and tonight would not be an exception. He stood, unbuckling his belt as he got to his feet. He could feel Blake's body heat radiating off her perfect smooth skin. Her eyes held no fear, only mischief like Jasper's. Jesus, was he the only one with any fucking reservations about the line the three of them were about to leap over?

Blake's gaze trailed over his bare chest, like she was suddenly seeing him in a new light. Because they both knew she'd seen him shirtless plenty of times. "What now, what do I—"

Jasper tsked behind her, his fingers dragging slowly up her side, rendering her speechless. Which was no easy feat. "You don't need to do anything. You don't need to worry about anything."

Jasper's words were so familiar. He and Riley had done this together so many times he'd actually lost count. For some reason the softly spoken words, words he'd heard over and over, helped him relax. Relax and remember his role here. He reached out, cupping Blake's cheek, his gaze searching hers. "You want this?" She nodded, like he knew she would. "Then all you need to do is trust us and submit."

At this her pretty blue eyes narrowed into a glare. "Submit? Is Jasper about to pull a rope out of his ass and tie me up? Do I need a safe word?"

"Why is it that all girls go there? Has every one of you read that *Fifty Shades* book?" Jasper snorted as he unbuttoned her jeans and pushed them down her toned legs. "Submitting doesn't always look like that, doll. There are no whips and chains here."

It annoyed Jasper every time a girl misunderstood their instruction. Submitting to them was simply letting go, letting them take control. It had nothing to do with a kink and everything to do with their wolves. They couldn't ever fully explain that to anyone they'd been with, but once they took over, there were never any more questions, any more conversation at all. "The only safe word you need is no. You want this to end, say the word, doll face."

Blake closed her eyes, leaning her head to the side and farther into his palm before nodding. "I trust you."

Jasper grabbed her hips, pulling her back against him and whispering against the column of her throat. "Both of us. You have to trust us both or this will never work." He ripped her panties down the sides, letting them flutter to the floor.

Her eyes opened, her head turning to look over her shoulder. "I wouldn't have said yes if I didn't." Riley knew that Blake's trust in Jasper was built on the fact that he was family, that Riley loved him. "I trust you both."

Jasper's smile turned wicked as he moved in to kiss Blake. Riley couldn't let him have it, he couldn't let Jasper kiss her when he never had. He grabbed her by the throat, spinning her back around to face him as he fused his lips to hers. She moaned, opening for him instantly. Tingles spread up his spine, his wolf finally waking up.

He'd had Blake in his arms, while they'd lain in his bed. She'd been wrapped in his clothes, his scent. Tonight was different. He could no longer see her as his friend, as the happy girl who pulled him out of his shell. Now he wanted her in a way he never saw coming. He swallowed the whimper on her lips, kissing her deeply, his hand applying pressure to the column of her slender throat. She was at his mercy, their mercy, and the anticipation was starting to kill him.

Riley dropped to his knees while Jasper starting raining kisses across her shoulders and up to her lips. He watched for a moment as his packmate devoured his new best friend. He waited for irritation to rise, for his wolf and human brain to demand he put a stop to this.

It never came so he put his hands on her thighs, helping her spread her legs and make room for him. He licked her clit, smiling against her smooth flesh when she fisted her fingers into his hair, spurring him on. He sucked her into his mouth, dipping his fingers inside her and spreading her wetness around. They didn't have lube, and if this was what she really wanted, he refused to let her feel one ounce of pain.

Jasper trailed his fingertips down her spine before his touch mingled with Riley's. "It's not enough, bro. Make our girl scream, then she'll be ready."

Riley picked up Blake, his palms on her bare ass, spinning around to lay her out on the couch. He threw one of her legs over the back, then dove back in, using his mouth, his fingers, and his tongue. He worked her pussy over while Jasper continued to kiss and suck her throat, her chest, her lips.

It didn't take long for her to shatter around him, his name whispered like a prayer. He raised his head, sat up, and then pulled her into his lap, positioning her above his dick. Jasper tossed him a condom and he pushed down his jeans before sheathing himself. His attention was focused on the gorgeous girl on top of him, her pulse thrumming rapidly in her slender neck. "You still want this? Want us both?"

She bit her bottom lip, glancing over her shoulder, watching Jasper get ready. When her gaze met Riley's again, she nodded. "Yes. I want you both."

Part of him hoped she'd change her mind, save them from crossing the next line. He reached up, grabbing her throat and pulled her to him.

He kissed her, pouring his affection for her into every stroke of his tongue. She mattered in a big way. She'd saved him when he didn't even realize he was drowning in his own misery.

He moved one hand to her hip, guiding her down onto his rock-hard cock. He used his hold on her neck to pull her forward until she was resting her forehead on his shoulder.

Riley's gaze moved to Jasper as he stepped up to them, his dick in his hand and an eager glint in his eyes. This was Jasper's favorite part, the moment they were both fully inside whoever they were with. He watched as his packmate place his palm on Blake's back, made her lie fully against Riley's body. He helped her move her hips, making sure she was feeling good before Jasper invaded her. The second a low moan left her lips, Jasper placed the head of his cock against her ass. Blake stiffened slightly in Riley's arms.

"You can stop this, baby."

She shook her head. "No. I want it. Don't stop." She spoke between panting, breathy whimpers.

"Come here, doll." He moved her lips to his, kissing her, thrusting up into her in small shallow movements. "Take a deep breath for me." She complied and he nipped at her bottom lip. "Focus on me inside you. It's so fucking good, doll face. It's perfect. You're perfect." She winced against his mouth while Jasper pushed in farther. "Jasper," Riley growled.

"I got it, man." Jasper licked his fingers, dragging them between her and Riley, playing with her clit. Riley could feel him inch in the rest of the way. "I'm in. We're good."

"Be careful with her," Riley warned. Jasper never wanted to hurt anyone, but if one of them were going to get carried away too quick, it was him. His wolf was always hungry, always wanting more.

"I'm okay, it's okay. Just please, don't fucking stop." Blake swirled her hips, her fingers digging into Riley's shoulders as they both started to move inside her. "Oh my god."

Riley and Jasper took over, working in sync to drag as much pleasure out of her body as they could.

Jasper leaned forward, his mouth on her spine while Riley kissed her senseless. He'd shared plenty of girls with his packmate, but nothing had ever felt as fucking perfect as Blake's pussy. The way she smelled, the way she tasted. She was candy, every damn inch of her.

She was moaning between them, the words falling from her lips no longer making any sense. Her body was shaking, her nails drawing blood. "That's it, doll. Just like that." Jasper wrapped her hair in his fist, pulling her up while he dropped down lower.

Her breasts were now where Riley could reach them. He sucked her nipples into his mouth, biting down, knowing how to bring her closer to coming apart.

"Fuck, I'm close, bro."

"Good." Riley wanted Jasper to come and get the fuck out of her body. He didn't know where that thought came from, his desire for Jasper to no longer be part of this. He'd never thought that way before. They always finished at the same time, they'd trained their bodies well over the years.

"You ready?" Jasper pushed Blake back down flat. She was screaming at this point, vibrating between them.

Riley fused his mouth to hers, swallowing the sound of her orgasm, loving the way she came apart. Jasper thrusted inside her all the way, stilling as he spilled inside her perfect body. Riley stilled, waiting for Jasper to pull out, a question in his eyes. Riley took Blake's hips in his hands, flipping her over and laying her out on the couch. He pounded into her, taking complete control. He'd never felt the driving need to possess someone so fully as he did the beautiful blonde staring up at him.

He buried himself to the hilt, coming on a growl.

Chapter Thirteen

Riley opened his eyes, blinking a few times to adjust to the dim light coming in through the few windows the cabin had. He was on the couch, his spine against the back, and Blake was plastered to his front. He lifted his head slightly to make sure that Jasper was still on the floor in front of the fire. There hadn't been room for three on the old sofa, and he'd had no problem kicking Jasper to the ground. After last night, he'd happily have made his packmate sleep outside in the truck.

Last night.

Riley closed his eyes, breathing in Blake's sweet bubblegum scent as flashes of images assaulted his brain. Blake on his lap, her back arched, her small hand wrapped around his packmate. Her breaths in his ear, her body tensing at the foreign intrusion. She'd come, over and over, until she'd fallen asleep in his arms. He'd held her tight, all night. Fuck. He'd had sex with his best friend. More than that, he'd shared her with his packmate. Two things that he had never wanted to happen.

"Stop freaking out, sourpuss." He glanced down to find Blake smiling up at him. "We're all okay."

"I'm not freaking out," he lied. Completely.

Blake laughed lightly, pushing on his chest to sit up. "I know you better than that." She placed a palm on his still-bare chest, her hair a wild, sexy mess of blonde curls.

"So do I." Jasper groaned as he turned over onto all fours and slowly got to his feet. "That floor killed my back." He glanced at the two of them on the couch. "You guys suck." He pulled his extra sweatshirt over his head, like he was cold now that the fire was dying.

Riley rubbed his hand up and down Blake's back, loving that she was wearing his clothes, loving she was always wearing his clothes. His eyes met Jasper's, communicating without words. "How do you feel, doll face?" His stomach was in knots, waiting for her reaction. "You, uh, need anything?"

He and Jasper didn't do sleepovers for a reason. The first few times they'd allowed it, the girls had woken up basically begging to have them all over again. They'd learned that repeating things the next morning only dragged out their connection, only made things harder on their partners. That was never their game. They never set out to hurt anyone. Fuckboys or not.

"I need…" Blake leaned forward, her nails creeping down his bare chest. "Sssssss…" She dragged out the letter out, moving to straddle his lap. "Sausage, egg, and cheese McGriddle."

Jasper snorted out a laugh. "If there was a magic genie in this room and you had one wish, what would it be?"

Riley swallowed past the lump in his throat. The feel of her core against his dick was making it difficult to think about anything else. It was taking all his willpower not to get hard as fucking stone.

Blake tapped her chin like she was contemplating Jasper's question. "Still the McGriddle." She sighed. "It's sad, right? One wish, it should be world peace." She held her hands up, surrender style. "But I'm starving, so I stick with my first answer." She hopped up and smacked a kiss on his cheek, then Jasper's on her way to the small bathroom.

Riley sat up and Jasper collapsed into the sofa beside him. "She doesn't want our dicks. She wants greasy fast food. You were worried for nothing."

"Was I?" Riley pursed his lips, perplexed at Blake's casual attitude this morning. "No other girl has ever reacted like that. They all want more. They're all a little crazed the next day."

Jasper had stopped giving out his phone number to their hookups, unwilling to deal with the bombardment of texts the next day. Which was why he called Riley good cop, because he continued to let them down easy.

"Yeah, but Blake isn't like any other chick I've met." He shrugged, buttoning his jeans and turning the ashes over to put the fire out. "Blake is cool. She reminds me of Axie." He picked up Riley's sweater from the arm of the couch and tossed it at him. "If we would've kept going and shared Axie that first night we met her, I'm convinced she would've kicked us out of her bed afterward."

Riley nodded, agreeing with Jasper's assessment. "Well then, let's go get her that damn McGriddle, huh?"

"Fuck yeah." Jasper put his hands on Riley's shoulders after he stood, shaking him playfully. "She earned it."

"I earned two." Blake came out of the bathroom, piling her hair on top of her head, a smirk on her pretty face. "One for each of you."

Riley sighed, relaxing into her arms when she wrapped them around his waist. "And you're sure you're okay? You don't hate me? You can hate Jasper all you want, but you can't hate me, okay?" He was feeling panicked all over again. She had become one of his best friends. She'd saved him back in Greenly. Riley knew he'd feel her absence like a hole in his heart if last night ruined things between them.

"I'm okay." She leaned her head back, staring up at him. "We're okay. Everyone is okay." She smacked his ass as she made her way to the door, pausing with her hand on the knob. "This all stays here, in this tiny little cabin, right?" She looked over her shoulder, eyes on Jasper.

He used his finger to mime an "X" over his heart. "It all stays here." His gaze moved to Riley's. "The second we walk out that door, this never happened." He waited until Blake opened the door and then chuckled. "Until I need spank bank material of course."

TEXTS

Blake + Riley

Blake: You okay, sourpuss?

Riley: Just got back home. I kicked Jasper out of my truck while it was still running.

Blake: I know you're worried about me, but I promise, nothing changes. Stop punishing him for something we all wanted.

Riley: He started it.

Blake: Yeah, but you finished it. Quite well, I might add.

Riley: I've seen you naked.

Blake: Ditto.

Riley: I know what you sound like when you come. What you feel like.

Blake: I thought we were supposed to leave all those memories back at the cabin?

Riley: You're right. I'm sorry. I guess right now I'm the only one making it weird, huh?

Blake: I'm memorable. You'll move on though.

Riley: Tell me again that you're okay.

Blake: I'm okay. We're still besties, and Jasper is as much of a jackass as you made him out to be.

Riley: You don't want him?

Blake: I don't want him. I don't want you. The cabin never happened.

Riley: Thank you.

Blake: Thank YOU. Two dicks? Better than I thought it would be.

Riley: Blake.

Blake: I'm kidding, geez. See? One day without me and you're already losing your sense of humor.

Riley: How is it being home?

Blake: Nice. Cozy. I missed my parents. I'm meeting up with some friends from high school tonight. What about you? What have you been up to?

Riley: Playing with my little sister, drinking beers with the guys. Home stuff.

Blake: Talk later?

Riley: Always.

TEXTS

Blake + Riley

Blake: You want to FaceTime later? I'm starting to forget what your freckled face looks like.

Blake: Geez. Leaving me on read? You're really sensitive about those cute freckles, huh?

Riley: Went on a run with Jasper. You still wanna see my cute freckles?

Blake: Hells yes. But I'm watching a movie with my parents. Rain check?

Riley: Sure.

Blake: Jasper looks like Wade Poezyn.

Riley: Who?

Blake: Cute model.

Riley: I just rolled my eyes really fucking hard.

Blake: Aww. Don't be jealous. I think you look like a young Michael Fassbender, before he started dyeing his hair.

Riley: I thought you were watching a movie?

Blake: I am. I'm watching National Lampoon's **Christmas Vacation,** *and I've seen this movie so many damn times I could quote the whole thing for you. So. Text away, bestie.*

Riley: I'm still mad at Jasper.

Blake: He didn't do anything wrong.

Riley: He knew what he was doing, dropping those hints in the truck. He's done it before, he knows where curiosity like that leads.

Blake: When he brought it up, he thought you two would be dropping me at home in an hour. Plus, it takes three, sourpuss. We all chose.

Riley: I'll get over it. As soon as we're back in Greenly and I can know that we're all okay. It's hard doing something like that and then being away from you.

Blake: It's hard being away from me?

Riley: It's hard not knowing how things will be the next time I see you.

Blake: Things will be like they were before I saw your dick.

Riley: Nice.

Blake: You were the one who said it stayed at the cabin, but you're also the one who keeps bringing it up.

Riley: I guess I didn't know how bad it would affect me.

Blake: I know my pussy is magic, but in time, you'll move on. Find new pussy.

Riley: Stop saying pussy.

Blake: Hahahahhahaha

TEXTS

Blake + Riley

Blake: Merry Christmas, sourpuss.
Riley: Merry Christmas, Barbie, doll face.
Blake: Miss me yet?
Riley: Immensely. What did Santa bring you?
Blake: Another dildo, thank goodness because now I need two.
Riley: Blake.
Blake: Calm down, I'm joking. You're so easy to mess with. What are you doing?
Riley: Packing, I'm going to stay at Jace's tomorrow.
Blake: Good. You and Jasper can kiss and make up.
Riley: I'm not mad anymore, we went on another few runs, it's helped.
Blake: Running solves your problems? Man, I wish running solved all mine. My ass would be a size two.
Riley: I like your ass the way it is.
Blake: Ooooooo is that allowed? Are you allowed to talk about my ass, or is that bringing up the cabin?
Riley: I didn't have your ass in the cabin, remember?
Blake: You got jokes now? You really must be feeling less stabby.
Riley: It comes and goes.
Blake: Like you and Jasper.
Riley: Good one, doll face.
Blake: It's weird not seeing you every day.
Riley: Well, all those clothes of mine you stole should help.
Blake: It's my privilege as your best friend to steal your yummy-smelling boy clothes.
Riley: Yummy-smelling? I thought I smelled like soap and pine trees?

Blake: Well, absence must make the heart grow fonder, but your clothes smell YUMMY. Probably because you gave me that good dick.

Riley: Stop it.

Blake: Hahahahahahahahahahahahahahahahhahaha

Chapter Fourteen

Riley was home, and he was so fucking happy about it. He'd spent a few nights at Dom and Corey's house. He'd rocked his little cosmic sister to sleep. He'd been the first one to go get her out of her crib in the morning. He'd marveled at how big she was getting. She'd even started walking. She could say so many words now. He hated how much he'd missed by being away at school. He'd needed a break from Jasper too. He was still a little pissed that Jasper had started that shit back at the cabin, although the text messages with Blake helped.

Being away from her was affecting him more than he thought it would. He found himself looking for her, searching out her reaction when someone in his pack said something funny or stupid. Missing her caught him a bit off guard, but it made sense. He'd missed Axie, Jasper, and Jace like crazy when he was at school.

He was the kind of dude who missed his friends when they were separated.

After Christmas, Riley had packed up and decided to spend the rest of his winter vacation with Jace, Jasper, and Axie at Jace's house. He loved being with his sister and Corey and Dom. But he found himself craving the closeness he shared with his friends.

"I don't know what we're going to do around here without Jasper." Axie came and sat on the couch between Riley and her mate's twin brother, resting her head on Jasper's shoulder.

Jace reached out from his chair by the fire, snatching her arm and dragging her over to his lap. "I have a whole fucking list of things you and I are going to do around here once his ass moves out." Jace nibbled at her neck, making her giggle and squirm. "And none of them involve you wearing clothes."

"Right, like you two have been so fucking modest the whole time I've been living here." Jasper shook his head. "I've seen your dick enough to last me a lifetime."

Jace grinned wickedly. "Good. Go to college and start staring at his dick again." He gestured to Riley before settling his arms back around his girl.

Riley couldn't help but stiffen in his seat. Jasper noticed and sent him an exasperated sigh. Like usual, Jasper hadn't given their night with Blake another thought. He didn't take anything too seriously. They'd agreed to leave it at the cabin, and Riley was the only one still having a hard time doing that. He wasn't mad at his packmate anymore, not really. He was anxious about getting back to campus and seeing Blake. He needed to know for sure nothing was going to change between them after what they'd shared.

Axie's eyes lit up brighter than the massive Christmas tree glimmering by the glass doors leading to the backyard. "Speaking of Riley's dick—"

"Really?" Jace nipped at her shoulder, punishing her playfully.

She laughed as she shoved him away. "I'm serious. I have questions, and I don't think it's fair I'm the only one in this family who doesn't know exactly what those two get up to."

"You've had a preview." Jasper winked at her, earning a growl from his brother. The fact that Riley and Jasper had Axie between them for a few minutes at a party once never failed to put Jace in a shit mood.

"You aren't the only one in the family who doesn't know," Riley interrupted before Jasper could say something else to piss off his twin. "We don't discuss our sex life with any of the pack."

Riley sure as fuck didn't want to discuss it with anyone right now either. He was feeling too raw, too scared of the repercussions of sharing Blake.

Axie shook her head, threading her fingers through Jace's to ease the irritation still pulsing off him in waves. "Not the pack, the *family*. Our little family." She pointed to him and Jasper, then to Jace behind her. "The four of us are part of the whole pack, but the bond we have between us when we're together like this... I don't know, it feels different. Stronger, separate."

Riley understood what she meant. He could feel it too. Riley loved his pack, every single member. But there was a certain ease to being here with Jasper, Jace, and Axie. "We're our own generation, I guess. Like Hadley, Allison, and all the other babies on the way will be part of another."

Axie leaned forward, her eyes dancing with mischief. "What would you two do if you ever found out Hadley or Allison, your precious little sisters, had been *shared* the way you two share?"

Riley nodded. "Kill the douchebags, immediately." He glared at the side of Jasper's head, remembering how badly he'd wanted to rip his friend's throat out when he'd set things in motion a few nights ago.

Jasper ignored Riley, pursing his lips while saying, "I'd rip off dicks and then heads."

Jace shook his head at their answers. "Do you ask them these questions to get a rise out of me, baby?" Jace placed kisses along Axie's exposed neck, making her lean her head back in submission.

Her eyes were closed, and she seemed to be more than enjoying his attention, but Riley could see the wicked smile on her lips. When Axie grinned like that, no good ever followed. "No. I ask them these questions because I *really* want to know if they've ever fucked each other."

Jace growled, biting her flesh again as she laughed loudly.

"It's time I move, man." Jasper pointed to his twin and his mate. "They are constantly all over each other, makes my dick hard. Then I feel shitty that it makes my dick hard." He sighed. "It's exhausting."

Riley polished off the glass of whiskey in his hand, then went to the bar cart for a refill. Axie and Jasper pretty much lived to fuck with Jace's uptight ass, and they did it well. Jace would miss his brother, Riley didn't doubt that. But he was also pretty sure Jace would be perfectly happy only having to deal with the crap Axie dished out on a daily basis.

"Well, you two going to answer my girl?"

Riley's eyebrows shot to his hairline in shock. "Are you serious?" He assumed if they tried to answer her Jace would fly off the couch and pull out both of their tongues. "You want us to tell her?"

Jace made a face. "Not really, but I'm tired of your dicks being a topic of conversation with my mate. So." He twirled his hand in the air, indicating they should get on with it.

"What do you think, *Rye*, should we tell her? Put her out of her misery?" Jasper smirked, using Axie's nickname for him. "She's been curious since day one, as you well remember." Jasper winked at Axie, pissing off his twin on purpose.

"Watch it." Jace's tone was low, a warning for his brother, yet again.

"To be honest, I'm really fucking tired of talking about us sharing." Riley sipped his drink, staring at Jasper, letting his newest round of irritation show.

"The answer is..." Jasper drew out the word, pausing to be dramatic and ignoring Riley's ire. "No. I've never fucked Riley and Riley's never fucked me." Axie slumped back, her bottom lip out like she was disappointed. "But." Her face lit up again as Jasper continued. "Both our dicks are usually in use at the same time, and if things touch in the melee, no one throws a fit about it."

Axie shrugged, like that answer was equal parts disappointing and satisfying. Jasper chuckled, but Riley couldn't even muster a smile. His mind went back to the cabin, back to Blake moving between them. The way her back arched, the way her lips parted as she reached for him. He didn't think he would ever forget the way the light of the flames danced on her naked skin.

"Huh, I thought you two boned." Jace shrugged casually, like he hadn't announced that he thought Riley and Jasper had been hooking up this whole time. "You're really close and, I don't know, I guess I assumed things got heavier than that."

Jasper's jaw dropped open like he was outraged. "Heavier than that? Excuse me, I announced I double penetrate chicks with my best friend and that's not enough for you people? Fucking rude."

Riley snorted into his whiskey glass, then headed toward the steel staircase. "You three have fun talking about my dick. I'm going to bed."

"Don't be like that, man, we'll change the subject." Jasper reached for his arm, stopping him.

"Will we? Because it seems like you can't help but bring it up whenever it suits you. Damn what I think, damn how I feel." Riley wasn't sure how he went from mildly entertained to pissed off so quickly. His moods seemed to swing all over the place the last few days.

Jasper hung his chin to his chest. "I'm sorry. I don't know how many times you need to hear it. But I'll keep saying it."

Riley shook his head. "I'm tired, bro." He didn't want to talk about his sex life, he didn't want to talk about sharing with his best friend, his brother, his packmate. He also didn't want to bring the mood of the room down or keep punishing Jasper for something they'd all promised to forget.

"What are you apologizing for?" Axie looked between the two of them, all the humor leaving her face. "What's wrong?"

"It's nothing." Jasper downed the rest of his drink.

It wasn't nothing. It was Riley's biggest regret, and the greatest night of his life. He was struggling with how the hell he was supposed to reconcile the two.

He pulled his cell out of his pocket as he shut his bedroom door. Whenever he was feeling pissed, regretting that night, talking to Blake always helped. She'd been pulling him out of his moods from the moment they'd met.

Riley: What are you doing, doll face?

He set his drink on the nightstand, collapsing on his bed, kicking off his shoes. He needed to get his shit under control. He needed to stop getting angry all over again. Blake and Jasper, they'd both kept their words. He knew he was the only one who hadn't come back to normal and let that night go completely. Riley didn't know why he couldn't seem to, but he was starting to annoy even himself.

Blake: Just finished dinner with the 'rents, taking a bubble bath to avoid family game night. My mom is competitive AF.

Great. Now he was picturing Blake in the tub, her naked skin covered with suds. He reached down, adjusting his hardening dick.

Riley: You're competitive too. You know that, right?

Blake: I'm a kitten compared to my mother. How's Jasper? You two go out and seduce a waitress for funsies?

Riley: Nope. I don't think we'll be sharing anyone for a while.

Blake: I'm hard to top. I should have warned you. I've ruined you both.

Riley chuckled at her text, feeling lighter now that she was joking with him. It was something he'd been worried about, her not being about to get over having him and Jasper. And here she was, laughing about it all like it was nothing.

Riley: I miss your dramatic blonde curls.

Blake: You should have stolen my clothes. It helps.

Riley: I'll remember that next time.

Blake: My mom is banging on the door, no more hiding. I'll talk to you tomorrow?

Riley: Always. Give 'em hell, doll face.

Chapter Fifteen

Riley woke the next morning feeling better, lighter. The tension was gone from his muscles, his teeth didn't automatically clench the minute his mind came to life. He'd gone on a run with Jasper last night after he'd gotten done texting with Blake. It helped dissipate the rest of the strife between them. Their wolves let loose, racing up the mountain and back. It reminded Riley why he loved his best friend, reminded him of everything they'd been through and everything they'd survived. They were pack. They were family. Riley knew his anger was borne of fear. Both Jasper and Blake had assured him over and over that everything would be okay, so maybe he needed to believe them. There was nothing he could do about it from Haxton anyway. Only the three of them being together in Greenly, starting a new normal, would reassure him fully. In the meantime, he wasn't going to let anything ruin the rest of the time he had at home. Riley had been looking forward to being with his pack for months, and he planned to enjoy them from here on out.

"Hey, man, you up?" Jace knocked on his door before sticking his head in. "We need to talk."

Riley's stomach dropped, all the ease he'd infused into his muscles was for nothing. He knew that tone, that hard look on their beta's face. Something was wrong. The lightness he'd experienced moments earlier turned to dread.

"What happened? Is it the babies? Is everyone okay?"

"Hadley and Allison are fine." Jace came all the way in the room, a tablet in his hand. "Who is this?" He flipped the screen around, scrolling, showing Riley picture after picture of Blake. There were images of them on campus, out at bars, dancing and laughing. There were pictures of Riley walking her to her front door, her kissing him on his cheek.

He felt all the blood drain from his face. "That's Blake. Why do you have those?"

"She yours?"

Riley shook his head. "She's a friend."

"She Jasper's? Because this one was from after you three spent the night in the cabin." Jace pointed to the one of her standing outside the truck with him and his packmate. They were all smiling, Jasper's hand on the small of her back as he helped her up into the cab.

"No." Riley cracked his neck. "She's not his either." He knew that no good could come from what Jace was about to tell him. Not with the questions he was asking. Not with the photos he had. "What's going on?"

Jace sat on the upholstered bench at the foot of his bed, closing out the screen, sighing like he was bone weary. "This guy we're going after, he's our last file to leak, and it seems he's one step ahead of us."

When Jasper had shot and killed his and Jace's father, a void had opened in the shifter criminal underworld. Jace and the others had combed through Franklin's files, finding dossiers on most of the big players in and around Colorado.

Jace and Axie took on the responsibility of leaking all the information they'd uncovered, which helped the authorities put away criminal after criminal for the past six months. They were almost done, which was the main reason Jasper felt ready to move to Greenly and start college. He'd delayed leaving in order to stay and help his twin.

"Constantine. He's a low-level mob boss turned drug kingpin after we took out Franklin. He's been steadily rising to the top of the food chain. Somehow, he found out he was next in our queue. That we were going to release his information tonight. I received this file an hour ago." Jace tapped the tablet's screen with his finger, bringing it back to life. "He's been following you at Greenly. In his email, he threatened Blake."

Riley had to clench his hands into fists to keep from punching a hole through the wall. "She's not part of this." How much could he possibly fuck up Blake's life? He'd already complicated their friendship by agreeing to that stupid night with Jasper, and now his pack drama was threatening her safety. Her life. "She's not pack."

"He doesn't know that." Jace shook his head. "He can't get to anyone here, we're too well protected and guarded. There's safety in numbers and he knows it would be pointless to go against anyone within arm's reach of me." He pointed out the window, like he inherently knew which fucking direction the UNC campus was from the bedroom. "You've been out in Greenly on your own, and now Blake is with her parents."

"She's in danger." Riley got to his feet, not sure what his next move should be but knowing he had to do something. Anything. He couldn't let them hurt her.

"She's a pawn." Jace held up the tablet once again. "If he thinks we're going to move forward, he'll take her. He'll use her against us."

Blake was a sitting duck, enjoying her time with her parents while there was a target strapped to her back. Riley could feel his heart racing, his wolf vibrating with rage within his bones. Neither of them was okay with what Jace was saying. It'd been a long time since Riley could feel his wolf trying to break free, trying to take over without his permission.

He could feel it now though. "I need to go get her. I need—"

"No." Jace cut him off, using his beta tone, silencing Riley instantly. "It's too dangerous, you can't be separated from the pack, you know that." Riley opened his mouth to argue, but Jace held a hand out, stopping him. "I've charted a plane to go get her, bring her to us."

"You want her to come here? Are you crazy? That puts her in the middle of all this bullshit more than she is now. I don't want her involved at all. I want her as far away from pack business—"

"There's no other choice. He knows where you live in Greenly. He knows where her parents live. He knows everything." Jace held up the tablet, shaking it violently. "That's what the pictures are saying, that's the threat. He knows our location. He knows our next move. He knows who we love."

Riley left that comment alone, because there was no point in arguing it. He hadn't known Blake long, but there was no denying he cared for her. "What about another safe house? I could take her there. I could tell her it's a vacation, spin it as something fun for New Year's Eve." Blake was always down for an adventure. She'd jump at the chance.

Jace shook his head. "He has pictures of the three of you at the cabin, which *was* a safe house. If he knows where that one is, he might know the location of my other ones."

"Maybe he had us followed from campus?"

"Not worth the risk. I'm not about to send the two of you to a remote location alone. A location that could be compromised, and you out there with no backup and no way to defend yourselves."

Riley knew Jace was right. Logically, he knew his beta's plan was the only safe thing to do. That didn't mean that he had to like it. His stomach was in knots over the phone call he was going to have to make. "I don't want her involved in this."

"It's too late." Jace's tone softened. "Call her, tell her to get on the plane. Tell her you want her to meet everyone. Tell her you and Jasper miss her."

"What?" Riley jerked back like he'd been slapped. "What does Jasper have to do with any of this?" All the jealousy and anger he'd pushed down over the last few days was bubbling its way back to the surface.

Jace glanced at the still-black screen of the tablet resting between them. "Some of the pictures, Riley, they were taken through the window. They're of the three of you, together."

"No." Riley got to his feet, his wolf rising, making him feel like he was about to crawl out of his skin. Someone had been there watching them. Someone *else* had seen Blake vulnerable, had seen her between them. The wolf inside him was a living, snarling thing, ready to draw blood. "It's not like that. It was one night. It was stupid and we should've never touched her like that."

"But you did." Jace got to his feet too. Being beta, he wouldn't allow Riley to tower over him. "Don't think I haven't noticed how strained things have been between you and Jasper since you got back from Dom and Corey's." He crossed his arms over his chest. "I'm guessing Blake is why."

Riley couldn't deny sharing Blake had put a strain on his relationship with Jasper. He was jealous, and he was worried. He'd had so many thoughts, so many concerns over the last few days his head was spinning. What he felt now, though, dwarfed everything else. He was rageful someone had pictures of Blake in those private moments. He was livid his life had leaked into hers and she was in danger. His wolf was about to lose its shit at the thought of Blake here with Jasper again.

Riley swallowed thickly. "She's my friend. Blake's not mine, and she sure as shit isn't Jasper's. That night should've never happened." He'd known it the moment his packmate and best friend had brought it up. He'd known that no good would come from it, but he'd let his lust, his curiosity override everything. Now they would all pay for it.

"Whatever she is, call her and get her on that plane." Jace turned toward the door, speaking over his shoulder. "You and Jasper can go pick her up from the airport."

"I don't want to lie to her."

"Then tell her something as close to the truth as you can. But remember, *you're* the one who doesn't want her in this world."

He'd had every intention of keeping his shifter life completely hidden from Blake. He'd made that decision from the beginning, and he'd worked hard to keep it that way.

Enter fucking Jasper.

Chapter Sixteen

After Jace left, Riley took his time getting dressed, dragging his heels. He was putting off calling Blake. He was trying to formulate what to say before she was on the other end of the line. Rehearsing his words over and over, tweaking what he could while trying to convince her to come visit. He had to be as honest as possible without further endangering her life. No big deal.

He was a little bit excited he'd get to see her. He was also a lot nervous about how things would be with him, Jasper, and her in the same space again. That was part of Jasper's sales pitch, they'd use Christmas break to get back to center after what they'd shared. When he was fully dressed, teeth brushed and hair fixed, he pulled out his cell and hit Blake's name. His stomach was a ball of nerves as the call rang twice and then went to voicemail. Before he could leave a message, his phone dinged with a text notification.

Blake: At brunch with the 'rents, what's up?

Riley sank back to his bed, his phone clutched in one hand. How did he explain the situation over text? He didn't have time to be delicate, he'd stalled too long. She needed to make an excuse to her parents and get to the airport as soon as possible.

Riley: I need you to call me. It's a bit of an emergency.

Blake: OMG. Are you pregnant?

Riley: How do your parents even eat around all your hilarity? Do they choke on their food often?

Blake: Let me pretend to go to the bathroom. Hold please.

It only took a few seconds for his cell to start ringing in this hand. He inhaled a deep breath before answering. "Hey, doll face."

"What's going on?" She was speaking softly.

Riley swallowed past the lump in his throat. "There's something I need to tell you, and it's not going to make a lot of sense, but I'm being as honest with you as I can possibly be, okay?"

"Uh, okay, you're kind of freaking me out."

Riley winced. If she was already freaking out, then what he was about to tell her was really going to send her over the dramatic edge she lived on. "We chartered a plane for you to come to Haxton, today, this afternoon. I need you to tell your parents it's a last-minute surprise for New Year's Eve, and that you'll be home in a few days." He paused, thinking she'd have something to say to that, but the line stayed silent. "Jace, Jasper's twin, he's not *only* tech-y. He's involved in some, um, stuff and he's helping put away really bad guys. One of those bad guys is fighting back, and we all need to go on a bit of a lockdown."

"I'm sorry. Is this a joke?" Blake laughed quietly. "You know how insane that sounds, right?"

"I do, and I know that it's a big ask, but I need you to trust me." Riley took a deep breath as he stood, pacing his room. "This bad guy, he got the wrong idea about you and me. He thinks we're together, and Jace thinks the bad guy could try to use you against us."

"Why? Why would he use me? I don't even know Jace."

There was no way Riley could explain anything further. He couldn't tell her about how packs work, or how criminals try to use mates as collateral. That's what was happening. Riley was sure of it. Riley hadn't been seen with any other females since before he moved to Greenly. Even then, it was random hookups. Whoever this dick was, he assumed that Blake was special, that she was *his*. They'd gone out together a lot. She stayed over in his dorm room. It wasn't a big leap to make.

"It's how this man works." Riley had vowed to tell her as close to the truth as he could. "They sent Jace images of us together, of Jasper and I with you at the cabin."

He heard her gasp, his stomach sinking at her discomfort. "Someone was watching us? Watching us together like that? Are you kidding me? I think I'm going to be sick."

He hated telling her that over the phone, he hated she was distraught, but he needed her to understand the seriousness of what was happening. He needed her to understand there wasn't another choice. She needed to get her ass on that plane.

"I know, Blake, I'm so sorry." He was sorry. He was sorry that her friendship with him had brought her into this crap, that her privacy had been violated, and worse, he had put her life in danger. "I need you to get on that plane. I need you here where we can protect you until the threat is eliminated."

"The threat is eliminated? You sound like a character in a military movie." She sighed. "Fuck, Riley. What am I supposed to do here? This all sounds so off the wall. I don't even know how to run out on my parents without freaking them out too."

"I would never put this on you if I didn't think it was necessary." He'd have given anything to keep her out of this side of his life. He knew he'd live with the regret for the rest of time.

"Shit. Okay. Yeah, okay, send me the flight information, I'll be there."

"I'll pick you up. Everything will be okay. I promise." Right as Riley said good-bye, Jasper walked into his room, his expression hard.

"Was that Blake? Jace told me everything. How is she?" Jasper leaned against the dresser, his arms crossed over his chest.

Riley nodded. "She's shaken up, but she's coming."

Jasper sighed. "And you? How are you?"

He forwarded the flight information to her, and then shoved his cell back into his pocket. "How am I doing? Well, I feel fucking terrible her connection with me put her on some asshole's radar. I feel sick thinking someone would hurt her to get to us. I feel uncomfortable thinking about her being here, surrounded by shifters. I feel irritated she'll be in this house, between you and me, so soon after..." Riley didn't need to finish his sentence. As much as he hated the thought, he knew the memory of their night with Blake was running through Jasper's mind, like it was his. A constant loop of steam and indulgence for Jasper. Regret for him.

"You think she'll ask for more?"

Riley shrugged. "Don't they all?"

It had nothing to do with ego, with experience or skill. Jasper and he were shifters. They were supernatural. Magic. Being with one shifter was one thing, but being shared between two? That was something altogether different. In high school, when they started such a dangerous game, they were both selfish kids. This was Blake. She was his best friend from college, and she was about to be locked into a house with the both of them.

"You going to tell her about what we really are?"

"No," Riley answered with more conviction than he felt. Jace had made a good point earlier, saying that the in-between was where Blake could get hurt. "There's no reason to tell her. All she needs to know is Jace puts away bad guys and one of those bad guys is fighting back." Riley side-eyed his pack mate. "And the two of us are both exceptional in bed. No supernatural abilities involved."

Jasper snorted out a quick laugh. "What about the pictures? Did you tell her about those?"

"She wasn't happy."

"Did you look at them?" Jasper smirked. "Jace wouldn't show them to me, but I gotta admit, I'm curious."

Riley glared at his packmate, growling out his response. "If you try to get to those pictures, I'll remove your eyeballs with a spoon."

Jasper put his hands up on either side of his head. "Whoa, bro. I'm in those pictures too. What's the big—"

"No." Riley took a step toward Jasper, his fists clenched at his side. "You don't get to see her like that."

"Again." Jasper crossed his arms over his chest, his relaxed façade pissing off Riley further. "You mean I don't get to see her like that *again* because I've seen it all, man."

Riley lunged at Jasper at the same moment Jace stepped into the room. He quickly put himself between Jasper and Riley, his arms out barely keeping them separated. "What the hell? Riley? Why are you fighting me?" He turned and shoved Riley back, pointing a finger at his face. "Stay the fuck on that side of the room." He looked over his shoulder at Jasper. "What the fuck is going on in here?"

Jasper shrugged, like his best friend hadn't gone after him moments before. "Not sure. Riley is acting *overly* jealous of our new girl, Blake."

"She's not *our* anything." Riley could hear the threat in his tone, the anger, but he couldn't seem to do anything to make it dissipate. Now that he was home, his wolf was living closer to the surface, controlling his actions. "She's my—"

"She's your what? I hope like hell you were about to say *friend*, because you fucking told me less than an hour ago she wasn't anything but that to you." Jace was back to pointing in his face again, his finger wagging. "I'm assuming if she was more than that, you wouldn't have fucking shared her with this jackass." He gestured behind him to his twin brother.

Riley knew he was acting possessive, jealous, completely at odds with everything he'd told Jace this morning. He hadn't lied to his beta. Blake wasn't for him. She wasn't his forever. He'd have known that by now, given all the time they'd spent together. Not to mention the night they'd had at the cabin. He'd been inside her. He'd had her. His shifter would have noticed, responded, tried to claim her.

He was acting like an asshole because Jasper was egging him on, as if he wasn't stressed enough. "Blake is important to me, but she's not *for* me. Jasper is being a shit, the way he always is, and I'm not in the mood for today, that's all."

Jace turned back to his twin, using that finger on him instead. "Keep your mouth shut, let Riley deal with Blake, and stop trying to piss everyone off. You hear me?"

Jasper nodded, his stupid smirk still in place. "Whatever you say, beta." He pushed off from his spot against the dresser. "I'll see you when you get home with Blake."

He winked at Riley, like the dick he was.

Chapter Seventeen

The minute Riley climbed in his truck and drove away from the house and his fucknut of a packmate, he felt calmer, more in control. Jace was right, he shouldn't let Jasper get to him like that. Riley was as much at fault as Jasper for what happened with Blake at the cabin. He could have stuck to his guns and said no. At some point he needed to own up to his part in everything that had happened. Sure, he'd had reservations, and he'd voiced them. In the end, though, no one controlled him except for himself. He'd wanted Blake, he'd been turned on by the mere thought of her between himself and Jasper. So, he'd acted on it. Now the consequences of that night were his to deal with, much sooner than he'd thought he would have to.

Riley watched as her small jet landed, impressed with the expensive piece of equipment he hadn't known Jace had privileges with. Mountain compounds, countless vehicles, computers, cameras…Jace's wealth was far greater than Riley ever realized.

The plane taxied in a semicircle, coming to a stop a few yards from his waiting truck. The door opened, the stairs descending to rest on the asphalt. Blake appeared at the top, in tight jeans and a loose cable-knit sweater, her gaze swinging to the open window his arm was hanging out of. She smiled and he couldn't help but return it. The circumstances sucked. Yet he was undeniably happy to see her. Never in a million years did he think Blake would ever be in Haxton, meeting his family and seeing the places that shaped him. He needed to relax and be grateful for the silver lining in all this bullshit.

Blake was safe, and she was here with him and his people.

He climbed out of the truck, coming around the hood to take her bag off her shoulder. He held one arm out and she snuggled into his side, squeezing him tight. He took a moment, holding her close, breathing her in.

"Well, I can cross flying on a private jet off my quickly dwindling bucket list." She pulled back, winking at him over her shoulder. He knew what she was getting at. Being double teamed was on that list too.

He opened her door, waiting until she got seated before tossing her bag into the back, and then he climbed behind the wheel. "How was it? Traveling in such opulence?"

"I'm ruined for all other air travel." She buckled her seat belt. "Have you never been on it?"

He chuckled. "I didn't even know Jace had access to a jet."

"Jace, Jasper's tech-y CIA-ish twin." Riley didn't love Jasper's name on her lips, but he was trying to let it go. "He's engaged to Axie? Right?" Blake wrinkled her cute little nose. "I should have paid more attention to how everyone is connected when you talked incessantly about them."

Riley pulled out of the small private airport and merged onto the highway. "Yeah, well, you didn't know you'd be sent for over holiday break, huh?"

"That's for sure." She pulled her knees up to her chest, hugging them and wiggling her boot-clad feet. "Are we in danger right now? This bad guy, how bad we talking?"

"Honestly, I don't know much beyond what I told you this morning." That wasn't a lie. Jace hadn't gone into detail about the newest and last criminal they were trying to put away, other than that he was a judge. Riley had been too stressed at the idea of getting Blake to Haxton to have bothered to demand more answers. "Bad man that needs to go to jail, he's fighting back, threatening the people close to Jace."

"Is he threatening Axie too?"

"I'm sure." What he meant was, he was sure whoever this guy was, he'd love to threaten Axie. She was at the compound, under lock, key, and Jace's watchful eye. He'd never get to her, and Jace would murder him on the spot if he so much as tried. "We're all going to lay low at Jace's house until the threat is over."

"The whole family? Everyone that lives in Haxton?"

"No." Thankfully, the whole pack wouldn't be under one roof this time like they'd had to do in the past. Jace had fortified everyone's security until he was satisfied with their safety. "Jace, Axie, Jasper, and us. The paaaaarty will come for dinner tonight though." He'd been about to say pack, but thankfully he'd caught himself in time. The dinner would be a ruse for a basic briefing of the now-escalated situation.

"I get to meet the people you missed so much I had to rescue you against your will? Score." Blake was smiling, her happy energy leaking through the cab of the truck and warming his heart.

He twisted his hands on the steering wheel. There was one thing they still needed to discuss. He knew it would be better to do it without Jasper present, for obvious reasons. "Listen, about Jasper."

"I know how nervous you are." Blake reached out, putting her hand on his shoulder. "I promise it's okay. I am not looking for a repeat, I swear. Things are weird enough right now. I don't want to add any stress to this situation."

"If you feel uncomfortable, or if he says anything you don't like, tell me, okay?" Riley waited until she nodded. "I won't let anything happen to you, doll face, I promise."

She smiled. "I know you won't, sourpuss." She turned to face him more fully, her feet dropping to the ground. "Now tell me again about this giant family of yours, prepare me for all the faces and dynamics."

"Okay, well, Corey and Dom have my little sister Hadley—"

Blake interrupted him to ask, "Corey and Dom, she's a counselor and he's a baseball coach. They're like surrogate parents, right? Your mom and stepdad don't live in Haxton."

"Right, Corey and Dom basically raised me the last few years." Riley wished he could put his connection with them and Hadley into words she'd understand. He'd vowed to keep her away from the supernatural side of his life, though, so her simple conclusions would have to do. "Keller, Linc, and Baze. They were all our coaches too. They are close, best friends, and they took us in. It's hard growing up away from your parents, but they made it easier. Gave us a family when we didn't have one."

Blake nodded. "Linc is married to Madden and they have a new baby?"

"Allison." Riley turned on his blinker, getting on the narrow road that would take them up into the mountains. "Keller is married to Molly, she's a yoga instructor, and they're pregnant with twins. Then Baze is with Pen, they were high school sweethearts and she's about to pop with their first kid."

"What does Pen do?"

"She teaches at St. Leasing, Madden is the school nurse, and Corey is the counselor. The only female who doesn't work on campus is Molly; she owns the yoga studio in town."

"*Female*?" Blake laughed, applying more of her bubblegum lip gloss. "You call them that to their faces?"

Riley felt a little dread pool in the pit of his stomach. There was so much that Blake was going to find odd, staying with them in Haxton. The words they used freely as a pack, the way they talked about each other. It was going to be hard for her to understand, but Riley would happily translate all day long if it meant that Blake would be safe from the dangers Jace and Axie were taking on.

"Inside joke." Riley smiled at her before directing his gaze back to the steep road. "We basically all lived on top of each other for four years. We have a lot of them."

They rode the rest of the way to Jace's house in easy conversation, talking about their Christmases and time with their families. Riley was happy to have Blake next to him, even if the circumstances were beyond fucked up.

"Jace owns this place?" Blake leaned forward, peering out of the windshield, her eyes going wide as the gates to Jace's compound swung open on their own. There was a sensor installed in Riley's truck, the gate reading his signature and alerting Jace it was him nearing the estate. Jace had to enter a seven-digit code to allow the gates to open. Their pack beta did not take security lightly. "How old is he again?"

Riley pulled his truck down the driveway, parking in his spot in the five-car garage. "He's our age, but he comes from money, and he's good at stock market shit." Easy explanations for a complicated situation. Jace saved every dime his evil father ever threw at him, turning it into a fortune he couldn't blow through if he lived two hundred years.

Riley got out of the truck, grabbing Blake's bag and then opening the door for her. He led her into the house with his hand on her back, laughing as her lips moved, counting cars. Jace had one for every situation.

Axie and Jace were in the kitchen, she was on the counter and he was between her spread thighs, his mouth at her ear, no doubt whispering dirty things. When she spotted them, she pushed Jace back and hopped down, a kind smile on her face.

"You must be Blake." Axie held out her hand. "I'm Axie, and this horny bastard is my fiancé, Jace."

Blake shook her outstretched palm, nodding. "It's nice to meet you both."

"We're sorry that you got dragged into all this." Axie leaned her head back against Jace as he spoke to Blake. "Thank you for coming to stay."

Blake shrugged. "Thanks for the jet." She looked around the large commercial-grade kitchen, taking in the Viking range and the custom soapstone countertops. "Your house is beautiful."

"You want a tour?" Axie stepped away from her mate, holding her hand out for Blake's bag. "I'll show you the room you're staying in and then help you get a layout for the rest of the place." Riley let Axie take the bag, giving Blake an encouraging smile.

"You can put her in my room." Jasper came sauntering into the kitchen, smirking as he picked Blake up off her feet, hugging her tightly before setting her back down.

Riley's jaw clenched so hard he was afraid he'd crack a molar. He didn't like Jasper's hands on Blake. He didn't like the image of them sharing a bed, let alone a room. His fists tightened at his sides, his wolf demanding he speak up. He shoved his jealousy down, trying like hell to remember Jasper was joking. He was trying to get a rise out of him. Jasper was being Jasper, and Riley needed to stop getting so fucking worked up about it.

It would only egg his asshole packmate on.

"We have plenty of space, there's no need to share." Axie eyed Riley, then grabbed Blake's hand and pulled her from the room. "Plus, Jasper still pees the bed."

Jace chuckled, the easy sound from his beta relaxing Riley's tense muscles. Jasper gasped. "That was one time *after* we drank a bottle of tequila." Axie's and Blake's laughter could be heard trailing behind them as they made their way down the hallway.

"Jasper, stop trying to make Riley lose his shit." Jace pointed at this twin before turning to the subzero refrigerator, pulling things from it for lunch. "We're all in this house together for the next few days, and if you spend them all fucking with your best friend, I swear I will beat the ever-loving hell out of you."

Riley and Jasper were used to Jace's threats, but Riley was glad to have him on his side. If there was anyone else in the pack who got irritated at Jasper's antics, it was Jace. Probably because the poor guy was constantly getting tag-teamed by his twin and his mate. They both lived to make Jace loosen up.

"I was being friendly." Jasper rolled his eyes, gesturing to Riley. "He's so on edge he's going to make Blake feel weird."

"Stop touching her like you have a right to," Riley growled, causing Jasper to narrow his eyes.

"And you do?"

"She's my best friend." Riley couldn't seem to get the low gravelly sound out of his tone.

Jasper crossed his arms over his chest. "And what am I?"

"Currently?" Riley mirrored his packmate's stance. "A pain in my ass." Jasper opened his mouth and Riley cut him off. "If you make one comment about a pain in Blake's ass right now, I'll rip your head off."

Jasper and Riley stared at each other, neither backing down, until Jasper started to chuckle. He stepped forward and slung his arm over Riley's shoulders. "I love you, man. I swear, I'm not after a round two. I know the stakes. I said I wouldn't do it again, and I won't."

Jasper's words melted away some of the tension that seemed etched in Riley's frame. He believed his friend, his brother. He was the only one, out of the three of them, acting out of character.

"I know what I'm doing, she felt no pain in that tight little—"

Riley tackled Jasper to the ground, pinning him down until he tapped out, laughing. He got to his feet, then helped his friend up.

Jace tossed some lunch meat out onto the island. "I'm this close to building another house on this land." He held up his finger and thumb, millimeters clear between them. "I'm about damn tired of having all you assholes in my space."

Chapter Eighteen

Jasper hopped up on the island, his hands gripping the edge of the counter. "You calling a meeting with the pa—"

"I've texted the family." Jace shot a glance at Blake, silently explaining to his brother why he'd cut him off. Jasper was going to use the word "pack," which wouldn't make much sense to the human helping Axie mix up a batch of batter. The girls had decided they needed cookies after the gourmet sandwiches Jace had made them for lunch. "They'll come for dinner. There's no use changing routine, right?"

Jasper nodded. "Right."

Axie and Blake had come back from the house tour, laughing and sharing a quiet joke. Riley was happy to see Blake getting along with Axie. That was Blake, though, always making the best of a shit situation.

"Riley, can I talk to you for a minute?" Jace jerked his head to the hall that led to his office.

Riley looked across the kitchen, checking to make sure Blake was okay with him leaving her alone with a virtual stranger in a house she'd never set foot in before. She smiled her reassurance, silently telling him she was good, so he followed Jace out of the room.

Once they were alone in his office, Jace closed the door and went to look out the large window that faced picturesque snow-covered mountains. There was nothing more beautiful than the holiday season in Colorado. "I really am sorry Blake got dragged into all this."

"Yeah, so am I." Riley didn't even want to think of his life without Blake in it, but part of him felt so damn guilty for allowing her to drag him into this friendship. Being away at UNC coated him in a false sense of security. He was separated from his pack, from the stress and the danger that accompanied the supernatural world. For a moment, he'd been nothing but a college freshman, waiting for baseball season to start.

He'd been more human than shifter.

"What did you tell her? How did you convince her to come to Haxton?" Jace sat at his desk, his fingers steepled under his chin. He always looked so collected, so in charge whether they were fighting off bad guys or brainstorming ways to take down the underworld.

"I told her you put away bad guys and one of those bad guys is fighting back. That we have people who want to hurt us, and those people have been staking out UNC." Riley straightened in his chair, letting his fingers tap the shiny metal armrests. "I said the bad guys think she and I are dating and I was worried they'd use her to get to me." He hadn't lied to her, not at all, he'd simply left out the supernatural aspect.

"She's going to be here for the week. She's going to be surrounded by shifters." Jace leaned back, relaxing a bit. "You think she'll be able to handle it?"

Riley sighed, shrugging because he truly wasn't sure how all this would play out. That was one of his biggest fears. "She's human. Like all the way, one hundred percent human. It's been a while since we had someone around who didn't already know who and what we are. Madden knew about shifters before she mated with Linc. She was friends with a whole pack. Pen and Baze bonded when they were eighteen, and Axie's father was a shifter."

Jace sneered at the mere mention of Axie's father. The man had treated his daughter like crap her whole life, slapping her around and kicking her out of her house as his final fatherly act. The pack had used him as a scapegoat, making it look like he was purposefully leaking information about his criminal clients. The last Axie heard, he'd gone into hiding. But the last Jace and Jasper heard? The man was screaming as they tore him limb from limb. It was the only secret Jace kept from his mate.

"You haven't been here, day in and day out. Baze has gone full-blown asshole alpha now that Pen is nearing the end of her pregnancy. He's demanding and possessive. He's even starting to irritate me, and that's saying something. You were on FaceTime when Keller announced he and Molly are pregnant with fucking twins, so he's a mess. These guys are all on edge. So again, what's your plan with your blonde Barbie out there? How do you think she's going to get through all this without some serious questions?"

Riley had to smile at Jace's description of Blake. Even he'd picked up on her Barbie resemblance. "I can keep our secrets. It's been done for generations." Blake wasn't someone's mate, and she wasn't born into this. "She's here for a week and then it's back to Greenly, back to her normal *very* human life."

"Well, that's not altogether true, is it?" Jace got to his feet, his beta wolf unable to sit for too long. "Her best friend is a shifter. After what happened between you, her, and Jasper at the cabin, she's pretty well acquainted with aspects of this life." Jace narrowed his eyes. Riley could feel him assessing his every reaction.

"What happened between us at the cabin has nothing to do with us being shifters."

"No, but we both know she noticed the sex was otherworldly, two dicks or not." Jace waved his hand in the air like that point wasn't important. "You ready to give her up? Make some excuse about why you two can't be friends anymore? Hell, you could let Jasper keep fucking her, he'd run her off eventually without you there to stop him."

"You are such an asshole," he said with conviction.

"It'd be easy enough, and you know he's probably chomping at the bit to get back in that sweet little ass." Jace smiled cruelly, his dark eyes glowing. Riley gripped the arms of the chair, his jaw locked tight. He wouldn't give in to this stupid game. "It wouldn't be a hardship. I'm sure he'd enjoy every second that he got to be inside your gi—"

"Stop." Riley shot to his feet, taking one menacing step toward his beta before he could stop himself.

Jace gave him the slightest shake of his head, making him stand down without a word. "If you don't plan to give her up, then you need to fucking come clean. She can't exist in the in-between, she'll end up hurt because she won't know how to navigate. She's human, I get it. But just because she doesn't know about our world doesn't mean she doesn't belong in it." Jace opened the door, letting the sounds of Blake's laughter filter into the office. "Figure your shit out. The pack meets tonight, and then your ass is going with us on a run. You need it."

Chapter Nineteen

Riley was sitting on Jace's back deck, staring off into the fading sunlight. The day had gone smoother than he'd anticipated. Blake was tired after the last-minute flight to Haxton. Axie took her upstairs and they spent the rest of the day in the master bedroom watching old movies. Axie told everyone it was because she was sick of being around boys all the time and was going to soak in the girl vibes while she could. Riley knew she did it to help them all out by keeping Blake from feeling the underlying tension in the house.

There was a threat, once again, to their safety. Not to mention Jace giving Riley an ultimatum.

When Riley had come out of Jace's office, Jasper was tickling Blake mercilessly, powdered sugar sprinkled all over the usually immaculately clean kitchen. Riley had immediately taken a step forward, his hand balled into fists. He didn't know what his endgame was. All he knew was he needed Jasper's hands off Blake. Jace had grabbed him by the shoulder, holding him in place while he did that silent communication thing with Axie over his head. She'd broken up Jasper and Blake by setting a fresh pan of cookies between them.

Riley didn't understand what was happening, he didn't understand his jealousy. He could tell himself it was because he didn't want Jasper to ruin his friendship with Blake...but the excuse was getting more and more difficult to believe. His feelings were an unwelcome surprise, to say the least. He'd spent the last three weeks of school with Blake, and he'd never felt jealous when she danced with other guys. Did shots with the basketball team. Flirted with randoms at bars. Never one single time.

There'd been no reason for it then, and there was no reason for it now.

"Hey, sourpuss." Blake walked out onto the deck. "Jace wanted me to tell you your family is driving up." Blake sat next to him, leaning her head on his shoulder like she'd done a dozen times before. "What have you been up to all day? I feel like I haven't seen you in hours."

"Catching up with the guys. Helping Jace figure out his next move." He lifted his arm, wrapping it around her petite body. "Did you have fun with Axie?"

"Yeah, she's great." Blake followed his gaze, staring out into the dying light of the sunset. "When did she meet Jace? They seem so young to be engaged and living in this dream house."

Riley was glad she couldn't see his smirk. They were young, but that was shifter life. When a shifter found the female for him, the one he'd spend forever with, age didn't matter. "They met over the summer actually."

"And they're already getting married? Wow."

Riley hopped to his feet, his ears picking up the sound of Hadley's little baby giggles. "When you know, you know, I guess." He held his hand out, helping Blake to her feet once she put her palm in his.

"I'm nervous." She stepped closer and pressed her forehead to his chest. "Your whole massive family is in there. All the people in the picture on your desk, and I'm going to meet them."

Riley laughed, putting his arm around her shoulders and leading her into the house. "They're going to love you, no worries, okay?" He felt her nod as they joined the growing crowd in the living room. There was a fire going in the fireplace, the bar cart was fully stocked. The whole scene made Riley feel at peace, even with all the turmoil going on inside him.

Corey smiled when she saw him, setting Hadley on her feet and letting her wobble her way across the space. "Look who's here, baby girl." Hadley followed the finger Corey was pointing at him as he crouched down with his arms wide.

"Come here, sweet girl." She giggled, flew into his embrace, and he peppered kisses all over her chubby cheeks.

Riley stepped back into place beside Blake with Hadley still in his arms. "Uh, this is my friend Blake. Blake, this is Corey, Dom, and Hadley." He bounced the baby, making her giggle again. She was such a happy little girl, always laughing and smiling.

"It's really nice to meet you all." Blake shook hands with Corey and Dom, then tickled Hadley's tummy. "And it's nice to meet you too, Hadley. Riley talks about you all the time."

Riley and Blake sat on the floor and played with Hadley. Eventually the rest of the pack started to filter in. The only time he got up to leave his sister and his best friend was when Madden and Linc came in with their newborn baby girl. He took her in his arms, rocking her gently. He was able to cuddle the newest member of the pack for all of five minutes before Jasper came into the room and stole his cosmic sister away. Riley understood though. He'd been that kind of obsessed with Hadley when she was born, and he never wanted to share.

Introductions were made, drinks were poured. Blake was still on the floor, Hadley sitting in her lap, and Riley was beside them. Jace and Axie were standing at the front of the room by the fireplace, Baze was pacing behind them while his mate Pen was in one of the leather chairs with her feet propped on the ottoman, her hands rubbing her rounded belly. She looked like she'd swallowed a basketball, but Riley had been around enough pregnant females at this point to know comments like that were best kept inside his head.

Keller and Molly shared a couch with Corey and Dom, and Jasper was standing behind Linc and Maddi on the loveseat, rocking the baby back to sleep.

"Okay, let's get started." Baze stopped his pacing, coming to stand next to his beta while Axie went and perched on the edge of Pen's chair. "Mathias got in and recovered all the information this asshole has gathered about our pack over the last few months, and he found out how they discovered the evidence leaks were coming from Jace."

Mathias was a shifter friend of Maddi's from a pack she'd met while backpacking through Spain. He and his people were hackers, virtual-age Robin Hoods. He'd been helping Baze and Jace for a while now, doing everything he could to assist them to leak the dirt they acquired from Jasper and Jace's monster of a father as safely as possible.

The whole pack had agreed it was best to try to take down the Colorado underworld as opposed to turning a blind eye on the corruption. They'd apparently been cocky, thinking that they'd be able to maintain the upper hand until they were done.

"Which is why Blake is here." Jace stepped forward. "These guys followed us here in Haxton, and they went to Greenly and tracked Riley as well."

"Why did you think it was best to bring her back here?" Keller shrugged, shooting Blake an apologetic glance. "Not that we're not all happy to meet you, but I don't understand why we needed to drag you into our crap, that's all."

Blake nodded in understanding, bouncing Hadley in her lap when she started to fuss.

"The photos and videos we found made it look like Riley and Blake were dating." Jace glanced over at Riley before addressing the rest of the pack. "We know from experience that people like this, people like Constantine, they go after everything they perceive as a weakness."

"Constantine? Is that this guy's name? You've been referring to him as asshole for the last week, so I wasn't sure." Linc took the baby from Jasper, wrinkling his nose as he sniffed her diaper. "Thanks, jerk."

Jasper smiled, batting his eyelashes. "Anytime."

"Jasper, change your sister." Maddi leaned her head back, smirking as Linc handed the baby back and Jasper moved around to the floor in front of the couch with a pretty pink diaper bag slung over his shoulder. "So this Constantine, you were afraid he'd go through Blake to get to Riley? I mean, are you guys dating?" She directed this question at him, wagging her eyebrows suggestively. The more time Maddi spent with Jasper and Linc, the more she sounded like them. That poor baby girl of theirs didn't stand a chance.

"No, we're not dating. We're friends." Riley smiled at Blake, trying to keep her from feeling uncomfortable in the middle of all this. "We hang out a lot. Basically, she's my only friend in Greenly, so I can see how they'd draw that conclusion."

"Why don't you have any friends, bud?" Corey's eyes filled with tears. "Are you lonely? You poor baby, I knew you should have stayed here until Jasp—"

"For fuck's sake, did you knock Corey up again already?" Linc leaned forward, addressing Dom.

"What? No." Dom paused, glancing at his mate. "Wait, are you pregnant?"

Corey rolled her eyes. "No, I'm worried about my boy. I hate the thought of you not having any friends."

Molly wiped at her cheeks, sniffling. "It is really, really sad."

"She has an excuse. She's got triple the hormones running through her body." Keller rubbed his hand on his mate's back, trying to soothe her.

"You guys, stop crying over me, I'm fine." He was fine, but his pack was making him feel pathetic, for sure.

"Riley could have had a million friends, but he stayed in his room like a hermit all the time." Blake knocked her shoulder into his. "But don't worry, I broke into his cave and dragged him out kicking and screaming."

"And now you're paying for it." Molly let out a wail. "You tried to help our boy and now your life is in danger." She shook her head, her shoulders shaking. "It's all so tragic."

Keller stood and lifted his mate into his arms before settling her into his lap. "You guys keep talking, I think we're going to be spending the next few months pretending Molly isn't sobbing hysterically."

"You had to go and be an overachiever, didn't you?" Linc shook his head at Keller, like he was disappointed in him.

"What?" Keller switched to stroking Molly's long straight blonde hair. "You want to point fingers at overachievers, how 'bout Dom? Knocked up Corey right out of the gate and threw everything else into fast forward."

Dom shrugged. "My wolf is virile."

"Your wolf is a fucking horndog." Linc rolled his eyes.

"Are you calling someone else a horndog? Isn't that like your superpower?" Axie crossed her arms over her chest, calling out Linc from across the room.

"Why do they keep referring to their dicks as *wolves*?" Blake leaned over, whispering in Riley's ear, reminding him she was sitting in the middle of all this and she knew nothing about the shifters gathered around her.

PART TWO

THE TRUTH

Blake + Riley

Chapter Twenty

Blake

Riley's makeshift family was something to behold. They were all gorgeous, they were all really touchy-feely and into PDA. But they were kind, and their love for each other and Riley came through in their every interaction. It helped explain a lot about Riley, that was for sure. He was such a nice guy, always a gentleman and never afraid to let his emotions show. Blake was happy that she got to meet them, even if the circumstances were a little hard to swallow.

Before leaving on that road trip home with Riley, Blake's life was pretty simple. She went to class, she partied when she had the chance, and she hung out with her best friend. Typical college life, exactly as she'd assumed it would be. Then, Jasper had entered the picture, she'd had her first threesome, and now she was hiding in a mountain compound surrounded by gorgeous males who seemed to be willing to step in front of a bullet for the people they loved.

Blake leaned over, Hadley's hair tickling her chin as she whispered in Riley's ear. "Why do they keep referring to their dicks as *wolves*?"

"Uh." He cleared his throat, shrugging one shoulder. "It's, um, another one of those inside jokes I mentioned."

She nodded, trying really hard to follow along with their conversations. All of this was so out of her depth. Blake knew crime was real, but the way Riley's family was talking, it almost seemed like something out of a movie.

"Can you guys please stop crying over me?" Riley sighed. "I chose to be alone. I was focusing on my workouts and my studies.

Blake literally barged into my life, completely uninvited. As much as I hate she's in danger because of it, I'm glad she did."

Riley moved his hand, putting it behind her back on the ground and enveloping her in his scent. She always thought Riley smelled good, like guy good. After she'd been with him at the cabin, though, his soap and pine tree scent seemed to trigger something inside her.

"Don't feel bad for your poor Riley, he has friends and Blake is a strong chick." Jasper picked up Allison and handed her to her dad now that she was wearing a fresh diaper. "We'll keep her safe until this is all over."

Corey glance from Blake to Jasper. "Oh, you've met Blake before too?"

Blake felt Riley stiffen beside her. Jasper licked his lips, like he was trying to hide a smile but came off looking wicked instead. "We road tripped home together the other day. I got to spend some time with her."

"Oh. That's right, the cabin."

Blake let out a little gasp, feeling panicked Riley's family knew about what went down between the three of them. She wasn't ashamed, and she didn't regret it. She sure as hell didn't want the people Riley looked to as parents to know though.

Riley leaned over, his lips against the shell of her ear sending unexpected goosebumps traveling across her skin. "They know we had to stay there because of the storm, doll face. They don't know anything else. I swear."

She nodded, her eyes cutting to Jasper, worry etched in his face as well. She sent him a small smile, letting him know she was okay. He was a player, and a shit starter, for sure. He also seemed to genuinely care for his family, for Riley, and for her.

It had been a long-ass day, and every though she'd been able to relax with Axie for a few hours, she was feeling exhausted and achy. All she wanted was to be back in Riley's dorm room, junk food spread out between them and a dumb movie on TV. She'd packed the clothes she'd stolen from him, so at least when she climbed into bed alone, she would have his scent to comfort her.

Riley thought she saved him, pushing her friendship into his life. The truth was, he'd saved her too. Riley made her calmer. He also made her make time for studying and actual sleep, so there was that.

"We'll work with Mathias, get this guy neutralized as quickly as possible, and everyone can go back to life as usual." Baze, she was pretty sure that was his name, was standing in front of the grand fireplace, commanding the room like a general. "I want the guys to go on a run tonight, the girls will be safer here, and then no more until the next time we're all together again."

"You guys really like to run, huh?" Blake played with the end of Hadley's silky hair.

Riley nodded, letting out a long sigh. "Yeah, we're all addicted to that runner's high." He jerked his chin across the room. "The coaches, they uh, hammered that into us in high school."

Blake wasn't sure how she felt about staying here at the house with all the girls in Riley's family. They seemed a little emotional. She was all for feeling cherished by the men in her life, but Riley's group seemed to take it to a whole new level. Still. She liked Axie, and at least she'd be here too.

"You want to hang out when you get back? You can pick the movie." Blake smiled as Hadley got off her lap. The kid was getting fidgety and was probably bored with the drawn-out conversation the grown-ups were having, and using Riley's body as a jungle gym.

Jasper sat down on the floor beside her, sandwiching her between him and her best friend. She'd promised Riley she'd leave the cabin at the cabin. Being between them though, she wasn't sure if there would ever be a time that their presence on either side of her didn't conjure up images from the night they'd spent together. She didn't regret what happened.

At the same time, she couldn't see herself ever doing it again with them or anyone else. Which was odd, because it'd been the actual hottest, most carnal night of her life, thus far. She'd gone to sleep on Riley's chest, knowing she'd want them all over when the sun came up. When she woke though, she found all she wanted to do was snuggle deeper into Riley's arms and fall back asleep.

"I'll watch a movie with you, Barbie doll." Jasper smiled in her direction. "Jace has a cool media room down in the basement with a—"

"Let's go, Jasper." Jace's tone was demanding, harsh, like his patience was running thin.

Blake didn't see the harm in Jasper offering to watch a movie with her. They were destined to become friends after all. They would all be living in Greenly together soon enough, and there was no way she'd ever give up her time with Riley. She wasn't even sure what her life would look like without him at this point. She and Jasper shared a best friend, literally, at one point, so they might as well learn to be buds.

Riley helped Hadley to her feet, and then climbed to his as he watched her toddle to Corey. He reached down and took both of Blake's hands in his, ignoring Jasper completely as he pulled her to stand. "I won't be gone long. You pick the movie." He placed a sweet chaste kiss on the top of her head and followed the rest of the men in his family out the glass doors leading to Jace's backyard.

"Have fun." Blake glanced around the living room, taking in all the still-unfamiliar faces. "I'll be fine here."

It'd snowed that day, and there was a layer of white as far as the eye could see. Not one of them reached for a jacket as they trudged through it.

Chapter Twenty-One

Riley

The run was good for him. It was good for all of them. Pen had told them once they needed to shift, they needed to let their wolves out as often as they could. It was what kept them a pack, what kept their old traditions from getting lost in this new age. Riley wondered what Pen would say if she knew he hadn't shifted once the whole semester he'd been at Greenly. The few times he'd come home for a visit, he'd gone out with his pack, but that was it. He had to admit that being home, being surrounded by the other shifters he called family, made his wolf live much closer to the surface. He didn't mind it at all. In fact, now that he'd been on a few runs he found he'd missed the constant companion lurking under his skin.

"We're going to grab the girls and head out. I guess we won't really see you guys until this is all over?" Keller was standing on Jace's back patio, his chest bare and his arms gripping the roof as he stretched.

Jace nodded, pulling his sweater over his head. "I think that's best, for now. Once Mathias digs in and we go after this last asshole again, we need to lay low."

Jace, Axie, Jasper, Riley, and Blake would be here in Jace's house. Baze and Pen lived a few miles away on Jace's secure mountain compound. The rest of the pack lived in town, all pretty close to each other with Jace's impeccable security setups.

"If anything changes, we'll let you know." Baze opened the patio doors, the sound of music and laughter filtering out into the yard where they'd gathered in the freshly fallen snow.

Jasper pushed forward, a wicked grin on his stupid face. Riley followed his gaze, his breath hitching in his chest. Axie and Blake were dancing, half-empty crystal tumblers in their hands. Hadley was twirling along, holding on to Corey's fingers. Maddi was twerking, holding her infant in her arms, laughing with her head thrown back.

"Your girls are a terrible influence." Dom shook his head, playfully glaring at Riley and Jace in turn. "My toddler is dancing to some explicit-ass music."

"Isn't Corey the one who taught you all the lyrics to 'Blow Job Betty'?" Linc danced his way passed them and into the living room, grabbing Maddi's hips and grinding against her ass.

"He's got you there, bro." Keller shrugged. "If anyone is a bad influence, it's your mate." He chuckled as he made his way into the house and helped Molly and her big belly get up off the couch.

Before long Jasper was inside, never one to miss an opportunity for a good time, dancing between Axie and Blake. Riley felt looser after his pack run, less on edge, less pissed at his friend. He watched the three of them, enjoying how much fun they were having. Enjoying the easy smile on Blake's face. He wanted her to be herself. He wanted her to let loose. He hated she'd been brought into this, and he hated that his unease about the night at the cabin was still lingering in his bones.

"A run helps a lot, huh?" Jace was standing next to him, his arms crossed over his chest as he watched his mate and his twin laugh together. "Dissolves some of the anger, the jealousy from taking over."

"I don't like hating him." Riley swallowed thickly.

"You love him as much as you hate him, so that makes it okay in my book." Jace cocked his head to the side when Axie bent over and shook her ass against Blake's. "Jasper would die before he hurt you on purpose, you know that."

"We shouldn't have touched her." Riley's words were quiet, whispered and drowned out by the music coming from the hidden speakers. "It's like he can't help but play the game, you know? No matter how off limits I told him Blake was."

"Did it ever occur to you that, for once, he wasn't playing a game?" Jace sighed, cutting his gaze to Riley. "Maybe he simply missed his best friend? Maybe he was jealous and confused as to why you kept her all to yourself? He wanted to understand what you felt, understand why she was so special to you, and he wanted to feel close to you again."

Jace's words hit Riley in the gut. He'd missed Jasper every day until Blake had come barreling into his world. Riley never once thought Jasper could be feeling the same loneliness since he was here with Jace and Axie, and was surrounded by pack. Riley been envious his friend was with their family when he wasn't. He never thought Jasper could be feeling the same emptiness he was.

"He's your best friend, man. He's your brother. He missed you the same way you missed him. He brought up Blake more than once, joking you were replacing him." Jace paused, snorting as Axie shoved Jasper off the table and made him refill their drinks. "Then he gets to Greenly, and Blake is a hot chick who you don't want him to fuck? Nah, man, you got him riled up and handed him a gift-wrapped ticking time bomb."

"It wasn't supposed to go down like that. That wasn't my intention. Ever." Riley wanted Blake protected from his life here in Haxton. He wasn't stupid, he knew that eventually she was going to meet Jasper. Though he'd hoped to avoid exactly what had transpired. Best laid plans and all that utter bullshit.

"You could've said no. You could've put your foot down. Jasper would have thrown a fit, sure, but he'd never have crossed you." Jace stepped through the doors, glancing back over his shoulder. "He loves you. Stop punishing him for something you allowed him to have."

Riley stayed on the porch, the cold at his back and the warmth from the house at his front. Jasper handed Axie and Blake fresh drinks, laughing good-naturedly as Jace grabbed his mate around her waist and hauled her into his lap and away from his always flirting twin brother.

Jasper slung his arm over Blake's shoulders, talking close to her ear and making her giggle. Riley swallowed past the new lump in his throat. Jasper's hands on her did something to him, no doubt. Sometimes it was mild jealousy, sometimes it was rabid anger.

Riley stayed in his spot, hidden in the darkness, half inside the house, half out. He was playing a dangerous game with himself, curious to see how he'd react to his two best friends.

He watched as Jasper took her hand, spinning her around the living room. He pulled her close, his palm pressed to her lower back sliding closer to her ass. Riley could feel his loose muscles slowly start to tense, the ease from his run dissipating.

Jasper dipped Blake dramatically, gripping her thigh and hiking it up to his hip. Riley's jaw clenched, his nails digging into his palms. He willed himself to stay put, to stay still. He needed to see how far they'd take their flirt. He needed to see how far he could be pushed without snapping. Blake laughed as Jasper righted her, those blonde waves bouncing around them.

Riley could smell her sweet shampoo, making it even harder to stay rooted to his spot. Jasper's fingers tightened on her hips, urging her to sway to the beat, both of them smiling like they didn't have a care in the world. Like Riley wasn't mere feet away at war with himself. Jasper's lips brushed her shoulder, his eyes closed.

And there was Riley's line. He could tolerate the touching, the flirting, the banter, and giggles. What he couldn't seem to stand was Jasper's mouth on her flesh. Riley stepped into the light, his chest heaving, his heart pounding. He wanted to cross the room and rip Blake from Jasper's hands. He wanted to drag her upstairs and lock her away, safe from his jealousy and his packmate's dick.

"There you are." Blake skipped away from Jasper, launching herself into his arms. She placated his bad mood without even knowing about it. Feeling her against him made the tension slowly start to seep out of his body. "I was beginning to wonder if you got lost out there, alone and shivering in the mountains, contemplating eating your own arm to stay alive."

Riley couldn't help but chuckle at her comment. So completely her. "Nah, those mountains are my playground, doll." He let her hop to her feet, looking over her head to Jasper. He spoke to Blake, but his glaze never wavered from his packmate. "Come on, I'll tuck you into bed."

Jasper rolled his eyes but held up his hands, surrendering to Riley's unspoken threat.

Chapter Twenty-Two

Blake

Riley followed her up the modern floating steel staircase, across the landing and down the long hallway with doors on both sides. Blake had gotten lost more than once today, trying to find her way around Jace and Axie's mountainside mansion. The house was gorgeous and the views were breathtaking. She'd grown up in Colorado, but there was something so much more majestic and mysterious about the woods surrounding the compound where she was being held. She wasn't a prisoner, and she didn't feel like one. It was odd, though, the threat to her safety, the need to stay locked away inside from the bad men who wanted to hurt Riley and his family.

Riley joked that Blake was dramatic, but her life had never reached this level of unreal. Criminals, secure compounds, safe houses, threesomes. Ugh. That threesome. She didn't regret it, because she rarely regretted anything she did. What was the point? There were no time machines, no way to go back and undo it.

Would she if she could? She wasn't entirely sure. She knew her night between Riley and Jasper had altered their friendship. She wasn't stupid. She could see the underlying tension whenever the two males were in the same room. The way they made her feel though was unlike anything else she'd experienced. Blake was pretty sure she was ruined for all other men, for the rest of time.

"What are you thinking about? I don't think you've ever been this quiet for this long since we met." Riley reached past her, throwing open her bedroom door and trailing inside after her.

She spun around, collapsing on the decadent queen-size bed. "Our threesome." There was no point in lying.

Riley groaned, perching on the edge of the mattress, his head hanging. "I thought that night didn't leave the cabin?"

"I thought so too." She crawled toward him, resting her chin on his shoulder. "So why are you irritated every time Jasper comes near me? I already told you I don't want a repeat, and I don't want him. Don't you believe me?" She was almost insulted to think he didn't. Blake wasn't into Jasper. Sure, he was freaking drop-dead gorgeous, like every other male in this damn makeshift family. She wasn't lusting after him, though.

"I do." Riley turned, his plump lips in a pout. "I know Jasper, and I know what's going through his mind every time he looks at you, every time he touches you."

"How is that any different from any guy, at any bar?" Blake wasn't conceited. She also wasn't one to deny her appeal to the opposite sex. Riley had watched her get hit on plenty of times, and he'd never seemed to care before.

Riley sighed, his gaze searching hers. "Because he knows what it feels like to have you. He knows how you taste, the way you sound when you come apart."

His words were turning her on, which she was sure wasn't his intention. She couldn't seem to help it though, his low tone flooding her brain with images of how it'd felt to be shared by them. The heat from the fire, the feel of their skin against hers. She took a shaky inhale, glad her sweater was covering the chills erupting on her arms.

"It's hard to forget, right?" He licked his lips, making her already-on-the-edge hormones stir to life.

"Yes." She wasn't sure she'd ever be able to forget their night together, nor did she want to. That was a memory that would keep her warm for the rest of her life. "That doesn't mean I want to do it again, Riley. I promised you, and so did Jasper. The only person who keeps bringing it up is you." Blake wasn't trying to be cruel, and she wasn't trying to upset him. She simply needed him to see she and Jasper were searching for their own dynamic, no ulterior motives on her end.

His eyes fell to his lap. "I'll get over it." He sighed, putting on a smile she was sure wasn't real. "We were supposed to have some space from each other, and that got shot to shit. It's an adjustment, but I'll get there."

"So you'll stop looking at your friend like you want his head to implode and his dick to fall off?" She grinned when she got an honest chuckle out of him. "He's a flirty guy, but I'm pretty sure it's all innocent, sourpuss."

"Jasper is a lot of things, but innocent isn't one of them." Riley let her pull him down to lie next to her, her head on his shoulder. "He'd jump at the chance for a repeat."

"Well, a promise is a promise, and I don't break those." Blake might be a dramatic ball of energy and flirty glances, but she was a good friend. She kept her vows, and she refused to hurt the people she cared about. No sex was worth losing Riley over. She wouldn't even recognize her life without him at this point.

She felt him turn his head, so she moved back to meet his gaze. "If you hadn't promised me, if I told you I was okay with it, would you want him?"

"Not without you." The words flew from her lips without thought. That's how true they were. They didn't even need her permission to exist. She reached up, letting her fingers trail across his lightly freckled cheek. "I wanted the two of you, the experience, not him."

Riley flattened her hand against his skin, his eyes closing and his chest rising with a deep inhale.

Blake rested on her side, her body touching his. "Can I ask you something?" When he nodded in response, she felt the bristle of his beard beneath her palm, which was still on his face. "Why do you share? Are you into him?"

Riley shook his head. "It's like we told you. A few weeks into our freshman year, we went to a public school party. They hated us, but they tolerated us all the same. There was a girl there, a senior. She was beautiful, cool, aloof. Every guy at that party was drawn to her, but she wanted us. We were horny kids, we didn't know the first thing about sex, but we talked a big game. She said it was the both of us or nothing, so we went with it."

"You were babies." Blake frowned, fighting the urge to go find that chick and beat her ass.

"We were." Riley scoffed out a little laugh. "I can see the wrongness of it all now, the alcohol she poured down our throats, the coaxing she did all night. But at the time, we were only thinking with our fourteen-year-old dicks."

"That's how it started. Why do you still do it?" Blake scrunched nose. "I mean, I get it, two dicks is hot as fuck." She giggled when Riley tickled her in punishment. "But do you ever, you know, go at it alone?"

Riley turned on his side, mirroring her position, palming her thigh when she threw her leg over his. Touching him was so easy, so natural. It had been from the moment she'd met him. She enjoyed being wrapped in his scent, his clothes, his arms. He felt like coming home, and she would never give him up.

"I don't know. I guess we sort of developed a reputation after that night. We liked it, it was fun, it was taboo and an adventure. It became our thing. Neither of us are into dudes. We aren't into each other like that. We've been with girls without each other, not often though."

Riley had told her from the get-go that his friends were his family, and Jasper was his brother. Those two took it to a whole new level. "Do you want to be? Or are you planning on sharing for the rest of forever?"

Riley's eyes seemed to widen at her question. *"The rest of forever*...no. We can't share forever."

"Does it make you sad? The thought of letting that part of your relationship go?" She tucked her hands under the hem of his shirt, using the seemingly constant heat of his skin to warm her cold fingers.

He smiled, pulling her closer and tucking her under his chin. "It'll be different, but no, it doesn't make me sad. All childish games come to an end, right?"

Blake didn't answer him, and she knew he didn't expect her to. She breathed in deep, filling her lungs with his scent. She felt warm, safe, protected. "Stay."

He hugged her tighter in response and she felt her eyes grow heavy. Riley had that effect on her. Calming her boundless energy.

Relaxing her without even trying.

Chapter Twenty-Three

Blake

When Blake woke up, Riley was climbing out of her bed. At some point in the night, he'd shed his shirt, his bare back a wonderous sight paired with his gray joggers. She would never set out to ruin their connection with something as trivial as sex, but she could damn sure appreciate the show.

She propped herself up on her hand. "Sneaking out? How fuckboy of you."

"I knew you'd wake up and announce how *famished* you were. I figured I'd go start on some breakfast." He pulled on his discarded sweatshirt, adjusting it to fall just right. "Was I wrong?"

Blake couldn't help but smile at how well he knew her. "Of course not. I'm so hungry I'm about to launch myself out that window and go take down a mountain lion a la Edward and Bella style."

"There it is, such a dramatic little doll." Riley winked at her on his way out the door.

Her shaky inhale as a reaction to her best friend was happening more and more since she'd arrived at the compound for safekeeping. Blake wasn't a girl who swooned, but Riley was certainly making her feel slightly light-headed these days. Still. Her convictions and promises to him and herself remained steadfast. Once they were back on campus, things would go back to normal. She was sure of it. Her fan-girling was merely a by-product of their circumstances.

And maybe the fact that he'd slipped so expertly inside her last week.

Blake fell back into the pillows, allowing herself a few stolen moments to remember her time sandwiched between the two Greek gods. Jasper was all sexy chuckles and ego, with the skills to back it up. Riley? He'd been like a barely controlled predator. She'd felt conquered by his touch. Slayed. He was rougher than she thought he'd be. He was the man women write romance novels about. Kind in the streets and kinky in the sheets.

The knock at her door interrupted her arousing thoughts. Axie's head poked into her room. "Do you want to build a snowman?"

Blake laughed. "What?"

"Doesn't have to be a snowman." Axie stepped into the room, twirling around as she finished singing the Disney song. "We're stuck on the compound. I thought it would be fun to stick a six-pack in the snow and build an army of anatomically correct snowmen. You game?"

"Hell yes, I'm game. That sounds like the most fun." Blake climbed out of bed, threw on some clothes, went to the bathroom, doing it all quick before pulling her blonde curls into a messy ponytail on top of her head. "I promised Jasper I'd go on a hike with him. Can we do it after?"

He asked her last night while they'd been dancing, after he'd gotten back from his run. She knew Riley probably wouldn't be happy about it, but that was all the more reason to go. She needed to make sure Jasper understood he was never getting back into her panties.

"Sure." Axie sank down onto the mattress, one eyebrow raised in question. "Only you and Jasper?"

"Only me and Jasper." Blake narrowed her gaze, knowing the real reason for Axie's cocked brow. "Riley is my best friend, and Jasper is his family. In a couple short weeks, the three of us will be back at UNC. I want to find my own footing with Jasper, not hop on his dick."

"Again." Axie's beautiful face crept into an almost wicked smirk.

"Ugh, they told you about the cabin."

"Jace did." Axie tossed the throw pillows into place. "He may walk and talk like a criminal mastermind, but he gossips like a little old lady at bridge club." She sighed, her hands going to her trim, jean-covered hips. "Can I ask you something?"

"You want to know what it was like? Having the two of them?" Blake wagged her eyebrows suggestively. She really liked Axie. They were two peas in a pod and instant friends.

"God yes. I want to ask you so freaking bad." Axie glanced down at her ring finger, her lips pouting as she wiggled the massive diamond, throwing sparkles onto the ceiling. "But my fiancé's head would actually explode if he ever found out. So I won't." She glanced up, meeting Blake's gaze. "Do you have a thing for one of them? Both of them? Or is it strictly platonic all the way?"

Blake understood the question, and the concern. Axie was looking out for the people she cared for, loved. Blake was doing the same thing. She sat back down on the bed, remembering their time in the truck. The ease in their laughter, the fullness she felt in her heart. The rightness of it all.

"When Jasper brought up that he and Riley share, I knew what he was after instantly." Blake rolled her eyes at how transparent he had been. "No one brings up something like that unless they're feeling you out. It's like guys who ridiculously talk about anal on the first date, you know?"

"Totally." Axie nodded, a shared look of annoyance between them.

"I was intrigued. I mean, the two of them? Who wouldn't be?" Blake believed people should try everything once. Life was meant to be *lived*. "But I also knew if Riley wasn't down, I was out. I didn't want Jasper without Riley, not for one second."

"So you're into Riley?"

"He's my best friend. I've never really thought too hard about why we didn't morph into anything more." It was almost as if they both friend-zoned each other the night they met. She'd been having too much fun to care. "Now, I'm too scared to lose him, to lose what we have. It means too much to me. I'm not a great relationship girl, never have been. I'd only screw us in the end."

Axie nodded. "I get that, believe me."

"Says the engaged chick sporting a diamond, a mansion, and a drop-dead gorgeous fiancé."

"I wasn't always this girl." Axie's gaze scanned the perfectly decorated guest room. "I was hell-bent on escaping Haxton, Colorado. I wanted to be free of this town and everything that tied me to it. I was a good time, a fun memory. Definitely not wifey material."

"What happened?" Blake was genuinely curious about Axie, about Riley's whole family. She wanted to know them. She wanted to know their history and their secrets. She wanted to belong with and to these people, the way Riley did. She was almost jealous of all the moments that existed here before she met them.

"I know it sounds so cliché, but Jace happened." Axie sent her a small smile. "The minute he touched me, I was his. He became my escape, my freedom, my everything. His life is here, his family is here. So here is the only place in the whole damn world I want to be."

Blake playfully rolled her eyes. "You're right, that is so cliché." She reached out and squeezed Axie's hand. "But it's also incredibly sweet and inspiring."

"Sweet and inspiring?" Jasper came into the room, launching himself on the bed between the two girls. "Are you talking about my dick?"

Axie popped him on the back of his head while Blake hit him in the stomach with a throw pillow. "No one is talking about your dick. Get out of here."

Jasper chuckled. "No can do. Blake and I have plans." He turned to Blake. "You still down for that morning hike?"

She nodded. "Yep. Just need some cold-weather gear. Axie, do you have anything I can borrow?"

"Downstairs, mudroom closet. Take what you need." Axie pointed to the door. "I'll scour the house for phallic objects while you're gone and then we'll start on those snowmen."

Blake high-fived her on the way out of the room.

Jasper was hilarious. Axie was a badass. Jace was a mastermind, and Riley was the best thing that she ever demanded be hers.

She might be locked in on a secluded mountain compound, but she'd never felt less like a prisoner in her life.

Chapter Twenty-Four

Riley

Blake never came down for breakfast, so Riley headed upstairs to make sure she hadn't gotten lost. Yesterday, he'd found her turned around in a closet when she'd been searching for the walk-in pantry. He stopped short when he came to Jasper lounging on the bed they'd shared last night, scrolling through his phone.

"What are you doing in here?"

Jasper glanced up. "Good morning to you too, bro."

"Where's Blake?"

"She's in the shower, cleaning my jizz from between her legs." Jasper rolled his eyes, like the fucking child he was. "She went downstairs, for fuck's sake. What is with the tone and the hostility?"

Riley's jaw was clenched, his heart racing, once again. He knew Jasper was joking, being an ass. As soon as he'd stepped into the room, he knew Blake wasn't in there. He had learned to sense her presence weeks ago. That didn't make Jasper's words any easier to swallow though. The images they conjured, the memories. Fuck. He was instantly on edge, fighting the urge to reach across the bed and choke the life out of his brother.

"You know you're the only one of us making any of this weird, right?" Jasper got up, tucking his cell back into his pocket.

"I told you I didn't want to do—"

"Shut up, man." Jasper held his hand up, halting Riley's clipped words. "We've been best friends, packmates, for almost five years. We've lived in the same space, shared the same girls, made the same fucking memories. Which means I *know* you." He stepped closer, irritation marring his usually relaxed features. "You can lie to yourself all you want, but I know the truth. You wanted her as much as I did."

Riley stayed silent, letting Jasper's words wash over him.

"I'm the bad cop, right? Fine. Make me the villain." Jasper shook his head, his eyes narrowing. "I could see the lust in your eyes. I could see how much you wanted to have that girl between us." He stepped past him on his way out the door. "I felt how hard you fucking came inside that perf—"

In the span of a nanosecond Riley had Jasper pinned against the wall outside Blake's room. His hand was wrapped around his best friend's throat, cutting off the rest of his stupid rant. Jasper grabbed his wrist, throwing it off and shoving him away. They were on opposite walls, chest heaving, staring each other down.

Which is exactly how Axie found them moments later. "What the actual fuck?"

Jasper scoffed. "Yeah, *Rye*, what the actual fuck?" When Riley didn't answer, Jasper threw his hands in the air and stomped down the stairs.

Jasper was dancing on his last damn nerve when it came to Blake. He was also right. Which had pissed Riley off more than anything that had happened yet. He'd wanted Blake, and he'd come so fucking hard he thought he was going to pass out.

Axie turned to him, arms crossed and hip cocked to the side. "You and Jasper going to really throw down? Or keep dancing around each other like little bitches?"

Riley sighed, leaning his head back against the wall. "Stop instigating."

"Stop telling us everything is fine when it's clearly not." Axie posted up next to him, turning to meet his gaze. "And I'm not instigating. I was mostly joking. The last thing I want is to see you fight over a girl with your best friend."

Riley knew he couldn't argue with that, couldn't deny that was what was happening between him and his packmate. Riley thought that he'd get over it, that he'd stop getting so jealous every time Jasper made Blake fucking smile, but apparently not. He couldn't even stand seeing Jasper in Blake's room, couldn't even take his stupid jokes about her in the shower.

"You guys shared her, right?"

Riley nodded. "At the cabin. Jace tell you?"

"Jace told me in Jace's own way, with as few words as possible. You know how much he hates talking about you two's wayward dicks." Axie wagged her eyebrows before sobering. "If what you three did is bothering you like this, why'd you agree to it in the first place?"

"I don't know." Jasper's words rang inside his skull, reminding him his friend knew the truth. "I didn't want it to happen, and then Jasper kept running his mouth. The more he talked about it, the more interested Blake got, the more okay with it I became." Okay with it was an understatement. He'd been drooling at the thought of having her by the time he gave in. "I'm pissed at Jasper, but I'm pissed at myself more. Now we're here, in this house together and—"

"And every time he comes near her, makes her laugh, touches her, you look like your seconds away from ripping his head off and bunting it into the woods for the bears to eat."

"Bit dramatic. I can tell you've been spending some time with Blake, but sure. Yeah. That's how I feel." Although, he'd had Jasper's throat in his hands and he'd let him go, let him walk away. Maybe he wouldn't actually try to murder his best friend like he kept thinking he would, not when it really came down to it.

"You aren't going to like this, but I think we need to go and talk to Pen."

Riley frowned. "Pen, why?"

"Your jealousy may be petty human shit, but your reactions are all shifter. Before the two of you rip my house to shreds, we need to talk to the one person who knows the most about shifter dynamics. We need to fix this, Rye."

***

Riley and Axie had pulled on their coats, and then hopped onto one of their four-wheelers to make the drive across the compound to Baze and Pen's new house. It mirrored Jace's in a lot of ways, with modern vibes and a lower profile. They'd used the same architect, who had been seriously vetted by Jace. The last thing anyone wanted was their blueprints and security details being sold to an enemy.

Axie knocked loudly, then walked in, announcing them loudly. "Please don't be naked."

Pen's laughter came from the direction of the living room. "No one is naked. I'm in here." Pen adjusted herself against the couch cushions a few times, almost as if it was impossible for her to get truly comfortable. "What's going on?"

"We need your expert advice on a shifter matter." Axie plopped down on the other couch, throwing her hands wide. "Riley is losing his shit and I'm afraid he's going to break my house when he finally explodes."

Pen's gaze moved to him, her eyebrows raised. "What's going on, bud?"

"Um, well, the thing is—"

"He keeps going all possessive wolf when it comes to his bestie, Blake, anytime Jasper gets near her." Axie glanced at him, rolling her eyes. "Or even her freaking room. Riley freaks the fuck out."

"Okay." Pen drew out the word, her eyes narrowed in apparent confusion. "Jasper is a player and Blake is your friend. I could see where his advances toward her would be upsetting." There was a lift to the end of her sentence, like she was still unsure why they'd come to her.

"This is the last conversation I want to be having with my alpha's mate, I assure you." Riley sat next to Axie, clasping his hands together. "But this jealousy with Jasper and Blake, it's more than that. He and I, we uh, shared her the other night."

"You shared her?" Pen's eyes went wide.

Axie shrugged, like this was a casual conversation to have. "They share."

Pen nodded. "Share. Share? Share?"

"Yes." Riley sighed. "We share. We shared Blake."

Baze walked by the room, growling their way, "One of you say 'share' one more time. I dare you."

"Baze, really? Stop eavesdropping. The kids came to *me*." Pen waved him away before turning her attention back to Riley and the issue at hand. "Okay, let me make sure I understand what's happening here." She adjusted her position again. "You and Jasper were together with Blake at the cabin, During the cabin, after the cabin, everything was fine between you and Jasper?"

"I was irritated at him for instigating the...togetherness. I was scared it would change things between me and Blake." In hindsight he supposed he should have been more concerned about what that night would change between him and his packmate. "I got over it for the most part, but now, I want to kill him. Like for real, murder."

"That started after Blake had to come stay here in the mountains?"

"Yeah." Riley thought back to the easier days he shared with Axie, Jace, and Jasper before Blake had needed to make the trip to Haxton. There was no real anger, no real jealousy. "The more he's around her, the less I can control myself. I want to kill him. I want to kill my best friend."

The three of them seemed to need a minute as his admission settled between them. Riley despised the newfound hate he had in his heart for Jasper. They'd been inseparable since they were fourteen. Two boys scared to be without their moms for the first time. They'd been through so much, survived so much. There'd been attacks, black eyes, death threats, baseball losses, championships, babies, and more happy memories than he could even count. Jasper was his partner in crime, his partner in all things.

"Is Jasper acting jealous at all? Possessive of Blake?"

Riley shook his head. "He's acting like Jasper. Casually annoying and hilariously inappropriate."

"That's pretty spot-on." Axie pursed her lips, nodding at his assessment of their packmate.

"And Blake? Does she seem interested in Jasper?"

Pen's question felt like a punch to his stomach. He didn't even think of that, didn't even have the bandwidth to notice if Blake was now crushing on Jasper. He sure as hell hoped not.

"No. I asked her." Axie sat back, pulling her legs underneath her. "This morning we were talking and I asked if she was into Jasper. She said that she never, for even a moment, wanted him without Riley. She wouldn't have gone through with the 'cabin' if Riley hadn't agreed."

He let out a breath he didn't realize he'd been holding. He'd refrained from choking the life out of Jasper earlier, but he wasn't so sure he'd be able to show the same restraint if he started hooking up with Blake behind his back, or if Blake decided she wanted Jasper.

Pen spoke again, jarring him from his thoughts. "Did you shift a lot this past semester when you were at UNC?"

"Honestly, no. I didn't shift unless I was back here with the pack." Riley knew Pen would have thoughts about that, and if her frown was any indication, he was right. "I don't know any shifters up there, and I never had the urge to run on my own." He often thought that was what might have fueled some of his loneliness while he was away at school. He missed his family, but his wolf? His wolf missed his pack.

Pen took a deep breath, her gaze going to Axie's before settling back on his. "Riley, do you remember how that old professor explained to Baze and Corey that as packs grow stronger, so does the pack mentality?"

"Yeah."

It was when Corey had first realized she was pregnant with Hadley. Riley and Dom's reactions to her pregnancy, the way Riley was connected to the baby growing inside her, had all caused a lot of questions to arise. They'd gone to a professor at St. Leasing with their questions. Riley remembered Baze being so annoyed at Corey because she kept asking if Riley had imprinted on the baby.

"Well, you've been away at school for a while, away from your pack. You and Jasper hooked up with Blake before you even got back to the compound."

In his mind, Riley felt like Pen was simply restating facts. "I don't get what you're trying to say."

"You're here now, in your territory, surrounded by your packmates. Your shifter, your supernatural uh, ness, is stronger here. Your desires are stronger here."

"My shifter desires?" Riley's eyebrows rose to his hairline, understanding settling into his brain. "No. No. Blake is my friend, that's all."

"You always have hot threesomes with your friends?" Axie scoffed at his adamant and immediate denial.

Baze growled from the hallway, "Please stop talking about sex around my mate."

"Baze. For the love of god, either join the room or go away." Pen threw an irritated glare over her shoulder as best she could with her limited movement. He snarled but didn't move. Pen turned her attention back to Riley. "You were intimate with her, right? You didn't just, um, watch?"

Axie giggled. "Oh, he participated."

"For fuck's sake." Baze finally came into the room, arms crossed and expression irate.

Riley knew what Pen was insinuating, but there was no way she was right. "We're friends, that's all. I'd been hanging out with her for nearly a month before the winter break. We've slept in the same bed. I've never once been jealous when we went out and other guys hit on her or danced with her. Nothing. I didn't want more than our friendship, or even thought for a single second that she could be my, uh…no."

"Riley, you hung out with her on campus, where you're most likely the only shifter for miles. In Greenly, you're more human than you are wolf." Pen winced, as if she felt bad for trying to implode his world. "Things are different here in Haxton, on the compound with your brothers. You're more wolf."

He couldn't deny that. In Greenly, he never felt his wolf, and unbelievably, he'd never really even thought about that part of himself. The moment he was back with his packmates, his wolf was back, always within reach. If Pen was right about that, could she be right about the rest of it?

Riley cared for Blake. He loved her. He hadn't asked her to come barging into his room, stealing his toilet and his attention. The moment he'd given in, though, he'd been a goner. Until the last few days, he only ever thought of her as a friend. Even after the cabin, he was hell-bent on keeping their easygoing relationship intact. Having her here in Haxton, in the house with him and Jasper, was tough. It'd been tough since he walked in the door with her, his jealousy running unchecked with a mind of its own.

No. Not a mind of its own. It was his mind. His wolf. His wolf who was skating so close to the surface now that he was home. Fuck. Pen was right. Blake was his. She'd been his since the night they met. He'd shared his fucking mate with his brother.

"I knew I should have never agreed to that night." Riley dropped his head in his hands. "I knew it was wrong. I fucking knew it would change everything between us."

"You knew, your wolf knew." Pen reach over and rested her palm on his shoulder. "Because deep down, you both knew Blake was always meant to be more than your friend, bud."

"Whether it happened in that cabin with Jasper, or six months later after some random college party where you both drank too much cheap beer, it was always going to be set into motion." Axie spoke softly, like she felt bad for the truths they laid at his feet. "You can't fight fate, Rye."

If anyone knew that, it was Axie. She'd never wanted this life. She'd been so damn close to freedom when she met Jace. They'd denied their connection, and they'd done everything they could to prolong the inevitable. In the end, the magic always won.

"I can't do this to her." Riley shook his head, because unlike Pen and Axie, Blake knew absolutely nothing about their world. Shifters were nothing but a movie legend to her. "I can't drop all this on her. I can't fucking flip her world on a dime. I can't."

"You've watched five wolves find their forever, their mates. You've witnessed it over and over and over again. What's the one thing that's true, every single time?" Pen's voice was soft, gentle, treating him with kid gloves.

"Possessive asshole behavior and a lot of growling?" Riley finally looked up, his lips in a thin line. He'd started in on jealous and possessive, for sure, but he wasn't growling. Yet.

"That. Yes." Pen's smile took over her face. "And. There's a happily ever after at the end."

"If she's yours, that means she's made for this life, Riley." Baze perched on the arm of the couch next to his mate, his hand stroking her hair. "She can handle it. The universe made sure of it."

The universe, fate, destiny. All that bullshit he'd heard the rest of his pack talk about for the last few years. He knew one day he might find his forever. He never thought he'd be nineteen and his best friend would know what she tasted like.

"Fuck me."

"She already did that." Axie snorted, then gave in and started to giggle. "Wait." She sobered instantly. "She already did that. Oh my god, Rye. She *already* fucked you."

"Axie, are you trying to make my damn head explode today? Is that your goal for—"

"Baze. I'm not being a dick." Axie got to her feet, pulling Riley up by the sleeve of his sweatshirt. "You had sex with her. You set your bond in motion. You're being a jealous ass, but her reaction? Her body is going to start craving the bond."

Riley's blood ran cold at what Axie was saying. Males became jealous douchebags, all possessive and dominant when their wolf wanted to finish the bonding process. Females? That was a whole fucking different ball game. Axie and Maddi had both gone through these intense hot flashes that made them fucking irresistible to the unbonded males around them. And the male most affected each time? Jasper.

Baze got to his feet as well. As alpha, he knew he'd need to step in and help. "Where is she right now?"

"She went on a hike." Axie winced. "With Jasper."

Riley tore through their house, out the back door toward the mountains, shifting with only his mate on his mind.

Chapter Twenty-Five

Blake

Blake followed behind Jasper, stepping where he stepped, making sure she didn't slip during their trek into the woods. Growing up in Colorado meant she was used to the snowfall. The powder-coated trees in the mountains surrounding Jace and Axie's compound were a whole other level though. She felt like she was surrounded by beauty and magic. She was glad that she came with Jasper, glad to have this time with him to establish an actual friendship. She really wished that Riley was here though, experiencing the quiet peacefulness she was walking through.

"Gorgeous, right?" Jasper paused, his hands on his hips and his breath coming out in a fog inches from his face.

Blake nodded, climbing another few feet to stop next to him. "It really is." She turned, taking in the path they'd ascended. Their footsteps were almost completely covered by the new flakes falling from the sky. "Thanks for bringing me out here."

He shrugged, sitting down on a fallen pine tree. "I'm glad you wanted to come." He worried his bottom lip, his gaze on his lap for a moment. "I know we all said we'd leave what happened between us at the cabin in the cabin. And I'm sure you've talked things through with Riley. But I just, uh, I wanted to make sure that you and I were okay."

For the first time since she'd met him in Riley's tiny dorm room, Jasper was showing a side of himself that wasn't cocky and playful. Blake sat next to him, knocking her shoulder against him. "I'm fine, thank you for checking on me."

"Riley isn't like us, you know? He worries and he regrets. He feels." Jasper hung his head a little lower. "I know he's worried about his friendship with you. I know he's pissed at me for starting things that night. I hate having him mad at me. He's my brother, my family."

"He has nothing to worry about when it comes to me." Blake had assured Riley over and over their friendship was the same as it was before the night in the cabin. She'd fight tooth and nail to will it so if she had to. "Out of curiosity, though, why did you start things? You knew he wasn't into it. Why'd you push him?"

Jasper chuckled lightly. "I'm an asshole, that's why. I was pissed he'd lied to me about you. I was feeling jealous and slighted. I missed my best friend. I came to surprise him and found he hadn't been honest with me." He picked up a stick, etching circles into the snow. "Don't for one second think he wasn't into it though. I know Riley. I know him better than he knows himself. He wanted you."

"If he wanted me, he could've had me long before the cabin." Blake rolled her eyes. "We've partied, danced, cuddled. Riley has never once made a move on me."

"Doesn't mean he didn't want you, doll face." Jasper cut his gaze to hers, his dark hair falling over his forehead in a casually cool way. "He never acted on it out of fear."

At that, Blake scoffed. "What did he have to be afraid of?"

"Losing you. Losing your friendship." Jasper stood, dusting off his ass. "Losing himself." He held out his hand, helping her to her feet. "We better head back down the mountain, I'm sure ol' sourpuss has noticed we're gone by now."

Blake let Jasper keep her hand, helping her climb down a few larger boulders, his words playing on a loop in her reeling mind. She'd never gotten the feeling Riley was into her, or that he wanted to take their friendship further. Was Jasper right?

Her initial reaction was hell no, but he'd known Riley longer than she had. Her mind went back to that night in the tiny cabin. The way Riley's fingers felt digging into her hips, the way his lips moved over her skin, kissing every inch of her. She took a deep breath, pausing to unzip her jacket. The mere memory of them together was enough to heat her blood. She felt flushed as she waved her face, trying to create a breeze. She tilted her head to the sky, letting the soft snowflakes land on her skin, cooling her down.

"Blake, you okay?" Jasper was a few steps below her, his forehead wrinkled in concern. "You're all red."

She nodded, taking off the heavy winter coat she'd borrowed from Axie. "Yeah, I'm fine." She wasn't about to tell Jasper she overheated thinking about the way Riley felt moving inside her. That was the opposite of leaving the cabin back at the cabin. Plus, he'd probably smirk and ask her what she remembered about him. She closed her eyes, clenching her teeth as a flash of Jasper pulling her hair up and kissing the back of her neck came unwelcome to the front of her mind. Fucking those two was like the acid flashback that never quit.

"Are you sure? You're kind of shaking." His voice was closer, like he was coming to her rescue.

The only problem was, she wasn't sure what was wrong in the first place. She wasn't a workout fanatic by any means, but it wasn't as if they'd been on a strenuous hike. They'd rested for the last five minutes and yet she was still overheated and out of breath. "I think, um, maybe I'm dehydrated or something? The altitude? I'm really hot. I swear, it feels like my blood is simmering in my veins."

Jasper placed the back of his hand on her forehead. She flinched at his touch, at his nearness. "You're burning up." He took her hand in his, and she had to fight not to jerk out of his hold. "Come on, let's get you back to the house. Maybe you're coming down with a bug."

She nodded, pushing aside her discomfort at his touch, and let him lead her farther down the way they'd come. After a few feet, Jasper stopped so suddenly, she slammed into his back. "Dude, what? Is it a bear? There's a bear, isn't there?" That was exactly what she needed as she fought the urge to take off all her clothes and lie naked in the snow. A bear trying to eat them.

"No. It's you." Jasper spun around suddenly, leaning in, running his nose along the column of her throat. "Holy fuck you smell so damn good."

Blake took a giant step back, confused as to why Jasper's hand tightened around hers instead of letting her go. "Um, yeah, I'm glad you like the smell of the sweat running down my back, but hold off on sniffing me, okay?"

He used his hold on her to jerk her closer, licking her exposed collarbone before she had a chance to react. He hummed appreciatively, the sound seeming to vibrate from his very core.

She shoved against his chest, trying to put some distance between them. "Jasper, what the fuck?"

"I can't help it." He shook his head, licking his lips.

She stumbled back as he advanced on her, unsure if she should laugh or straight-out panic. This couldn't be real, could it? Jasper wasn't about to overpower her in the middle of the woods above his brother's house. He was Riley's family. They were becoming friends. Friends took no for an answer. Friends honored your wishes. What the hell happened in the last five minutes? He went from concerned and wanting to help her down the mountain to stalking her back up it.

And he *was* stalking her, she felt like prey.

"Jasper, please, I—"

Before she could get another word out, a giant rust-colored dog launched itself at Jasper, knocking him onto his ass. The dog was growling, snapping. Blake stood stock-still, afraid to draw attention to herself, afraid that it'd turn his aggression on her instead. First Jasper went nuts and licked the sweat from her neck, and now they were about to be eaten by a feral dog. Fucking fantastic day she was having. She should have skipped the hike. She'd be safely at the house, buzzed and carving dicks out of the snow for Axie's project.

Jasper was on the ground and how he wasn't screaming for help was beyond her. The dog was still growling, snarling with its teeth bared and the hair on its back raised. Blake took a step back, wincing when she stepped on that stupid stick Jasper had been playing with. The dog's large head whipped around, his eyes locking on hers. She held her hands up, hating the way they shook out of fear. She was pretty sure she wasn't supposed to appear weak in this situation. Or was it the opposite? Was she supposed to curl into a ball on the ground? No. Wait. That was a bear. Fuck.

The dog stopped snapping at Jasper and instead made its way toward her, its head hanging lower and its tail wagging. She was frozen on the spot, afraid if she ran, it would chase her.

She made a vow to research some basic safety tips if she made it out of this encounter unscathed. The dog rubbed its head against her thigh, whimpering softly. She hadn't grown up with pets, but she knew enough about dogs to know that was a friendly gesture. Blake slowly lowered her hand to its back, tentatively stroking its thick fur. It rested its weight against her, allowing her finally to let out the breath she'd been holding.

Jasper got to his feet, breaking the small moment of peace between her and the big dog. It suddenly whipped its head around, growling at Jasper. Blake narrowed her eyes, taken aback by its reaction. Could it sense that she'd been wary of him only moments ago? She supposed it could feel the tension in the air. Animals could detect cancer and sniff out drugs, they sensed when seizures were coming. Surely it wasn't far-fetched to think this dog had known that she'd been afraid of Jasper's actions.

Blake put her hand back on the dog's back, lightly, nervous to upset it. "It's okay, buddy." She wrinkled her nose, leaning back to check out the dog's back end. "Yep. You're a boy all right." She patted him again. "You should go," she told Jasper, who was standing against a tree, his eyes narrowed on the dog who was still resting against her thigh. "It clearly has something against men."

The dog scoffed and Blake rolled her eyes. "Maybe it has something against dudes who scare girls in the woods?"

"Blake. Fuck." Jasper hung his head, drawing and letting out a deep breath. "It's not, that wasn't…Fuck. It's not what you think, okay? I'm sorry I scared you, I swear, it'll never happen again." He gestured to the dog stationed between them. "Head back to the house, he'll follow you."

Blake scoffed. "Why would it follow me? Is this Jace's dog?" She had been at the house for days and hadn't seen even a hint of Jace and Axie having a pet.

"No." Jasper sneered at the dog in question. "Clearly, he's a stray."

She peered down at her hands petting the russet fur. He seemed clean and well cared for. She had no clue what kind of dog he could be, all she knew was he was bigger than any dog she'd been around before. "Don't follow me, Jasper. I'm still skeeved out by your shit."

He held his hands up. "Totally get it."

She made her way past him, grateful when he didn't try to lick or sniff her again. Like he'd said it would, the dog followed after her, making sure to stay between her and Jasper.

She was already going through what had happened in her mind, wondering what the hell it was and if she should share any of it with Riley. He was already on edge about her and Jasper. Knowing his friend had acted so fucking weird when he had her in the middle of the woods would for sure make the situation worse.

"Blake?" She paused, looking over her shoulder when Jasper called out to her. "It's not a dog, it's a wolf."

Chapter Twenty-Six

Blake

Blake made her way back to the house, breathing a sigh of relief when the short gate separating the woods from Jace's backyard came into view. The wolf-dog was still beside her, brushing against her thigh every few steps. She refused to believe some lone wild wolf decided to rescue her and help her down the mountain. It had to be some kind of wolf-dog hybrid. Someone's pet who got lost in the wilderness. She was grateful for him either way. She'd been going over Jasper's strange behavior, trying to make sense of what happened. She couldn't. She'd started to feel flushed, woozy almost. He'd been concerned, and then he'd fucking licked her. She was all for some kink, but uninvited licking was not her jam.

Blake pushed open the gate, looking over her shoulder again, making sure Jasper wasn't following her. She wasn't ready to talk things out with him. She didn't know if she should tell Riley what happened. Hell, she wasn't even sure what *had* happened. She was feeling better now though. She'd removed her coat and gloves, letting the cold air bring her body temperature back to normal. She closed the gate after the wolf-dog casually trailed behind her into the backyard, like he'd been there a hundred times before. She hoped Axie and Jace were animal lovers.

Blake followed the sound of laughter, rounding the corner to find Axie shaping a giant cock made of snow. Jace was shaking his head at her antics, a smile on his face. There were three snowmen complete and a case of beer buried in the snow.

"Hey. So I made a friend." Blake reached down, putting her hand on the top of the animal's head as he sat beside her. Axie and Jace both turned and went silent. Axie bit her lips together, like she was trying not to giggle. Jace had his gaze narrowed on the wolf-dog, his hands going to his hips. "Things got weird on the mountain and then this dog came out of nowhere, helped me make it back down."

"It's a wolf." Jace sighed, reaching down into the snow and pulling out a beer, cracking the tab and taking a long swallow. "It's a motherfucking wolf."

Axie snorted out a laugh before covering her mouth with her gloved hand. "Where's Jasper?"

Blake moved a few feet away, sitting on a bench that was positioned by a silent fountain. The wolf followed her, sitting with his warm fur against her legs. "I don't know where he is, my new bestie and I left him behind." She accepted the opened beer Axie passed her. "I started feeling sort of sick, and then Jasper licked me."

"Sick?" Axie cocked her head to the side, like she was studying Blake, searching for signs of illness.

Blake shrugged. "I don't know what it was. I got really hot all of a sudden. It was like my blood was on fire."

Jace nodded, lips pursed, then drained the rest of his beer. He reached into the snow once again, opening another one.

Axie ignored him. "Jasper licked you, huh? Anything else?"

"He sniffed me." Blake shivered, feeling grossed out by the memory alone. Although she wasn't entirely sure why. Jasper had done a hell of a lot more than lick her back at the cabin and she hadn't been disgusted. Nope. She'd been begging for more.

"And you, um, didn't like it?" Axie's eyebrows raised in question.

Blake wrinkled her nose. "No. I didn't." She reached out, stroking the wolf's fur. "It felt—"

"Wrong." Axie's tone was sympathetic as she answered for her.

Blake nodded. "Yeah, wrong." She kept petting the large animal who had come to her rescue, smiling when it nuzzled into her touch. "Then this guy," she patted the wolf-dog's head, "came out of nowhere, growling and keeping himself between me and Jasper. Have you ever seen him before?"

Jace sighed, rather violently sticking a carrot into the face of one of Axie's snowmen. "Yeah, I've seen him around. He's super domesticated for a wild animal. He's a pussy." Jace threw a glance over his shoulder to the animal that seemed glued to her side. "You know, for a wolf."

The wolf-dog let out a low growl and Axie snorted beer out her nose.

"Uh, okay." Blake was mildly offended for her new doggy friend. He'd saved her. He'd helped her. He deserved her allegiance. "He seems to like me. You mind if he sticks around?"

"He can stay outside. He might have fleas." Jace sent the wolf-dog a smug smirk. "We'll get him some food and water though, put it on the porch with a dog bed for as long as he decides to hang around."

"Okay, thanks." Blake got to her feet, patting the wolf-dog on the head. "What should I do about Jasper? Should I tell Riley what happened?"

"I'll tell Riley myself." Blake stiffened at the sound of Jasper's voice behind her. The wolf-dog leaned closer, letting out a low growl when Jasper rounded the corner and came into view. "I'm really sorry, Blake, I stepped over a line. I can't explain what happened, but *please* know I'm incredibly fucking sorry."

She thought seeing him again would bring back all those feelings of disgust, irritation, and fear. Instead, she felt nothing. She wasn't unhappy to see him; in fact, she found that she was glad he'd made it down the mountain in one piece. What the hell was going on with her? She was giving herself whiplash.

"I'll go, um, find him and tell him what I did." Jasper moved past her, narrowing his gaze on the wolf-dog for a moment. "Are you feeling okay now?"

She nodded, staying quiet as he made his way to the house.

When it was the three of them, and the wolf-dog, Blake sank back down on the bench, drinking her ice-cold beer. "I thought I would be pissed when I saw him." She smiled when the wolf-dog put his head on her lap. She'd never had a dog before, and she knew he couldn't come live in the dorms with her, but maybe Jace and Axie could keep an eye on him until she could move off campus. She turned to Jace, a hopeful smile on her face. "If I check him for fleas, can he come inside?"

Jace studied the wolf-dog. "He looks mangy to me."

The animal left her side for the first time, trotting to close the distance between her and the others before lifting his leg and peeing on the snowman closest to Jace, sending some splatter onto his boots.

Chapter Twenty-Seven

Riley

Blake built another snowman with Axie, laughing and drinking beer with part of his pack. Riley hadn't spent this much time in wolf form in months, but he didn't want to trot back into the woods and shift. He didn't have any clothes, and he was pretty sure Blake had grown attached to him in the last hour. He lay in the snow, watching her let loose and have fun with Jace and Axie. Thankfully, Jasper stayed inside. Riley knew Jasper's reaction to Blake on the mountain wasn't anything he could control. His wolf was an actual horndog, and Blake's body craving the bond was making Jasper act in a way he never would've otherwise. Riley felt sorry for him. That was three times his wolf had made him react like a fucking asshole. Madden, Axie, and now Blake. Three females Riley knew Jasper loved and would protect to the death.

Riley might've been snarling and snapping when he'd lunged between them, but his anger had fizzled when the fog of jealous protectiveness cleared. Blake's body was under control and he'd heard the regret and remorse in Jasper's tone before he'd sulked into the house.

After talking to Pen, and seeing Blake have the same hot flashes Madden and Axie had before they were bonded, Riley thought he'd be reeling at the realization she'd begun to bond with him. There was no denying it. Blake was his, she was meant to be his forever.

Instead of feeling like he'd gotten hit upside the head with a two-by-four, with nails in it, he felt at peace, calm. The only part about all this that was going to suck major dick was telling Blake. Unlike Madden, Pen, and Axie, Blake knew absolutely nothing about shifters. She didn't know they existed. And she sure as fuck didn't know they mated for life. Her world was about to be thrown into another orbit.

Riley needed to talk to Dom and Keller, since their mates went through the same thing. Corey and Molly were human, completely and wholly unaware magic was real and was part of the men they loved.

"I'm freezing. I'm going to go track down Riley and make sure he didn't murder Jasper." Blake picked up her empty beer bottles, trudging through the snow to stoop and pet his head.

"Check the basement. I think Riley was going to get a workout in," Jace said, his gaze meeting Riley's wolf's.

"Thanks." Blake dipped down, placing a sweet kiss on his muzzle before whispering, "I'll sneak you into the house tonight. You can sleep with me." Riley leaned into her, resting his head against hers. Leave it to Blake to try to make a wild wolf an inside pet.

Riley got to his feet and trotted over to Jace and Axie.

"She's gone, shift back and we'll shove your ass through the basement window." Jace stepped to the house, pushing the long, low window open. "It's a bit of a fall, but maybe it'll knock some fucking sense into your stupid red head."

Riley shifted, stretching his back and cracking his neck. He was covering his junk with his hands, knowing Jace would not be happy about Axie getting an eyeful. "Sense? What the hell else was I supposed to do? She was on that mountain alone with Jasper." Riley knelt down and put his legs through the open window. "What I was afraid of happening was actually happening. He licked her."

"Your dumb ass needs to grab your fucking jackoff of a bestie and meet me in my office." Jace shoved him through the small space, not caring whether he landed on the floor in a heap. "Now."

Riley didn't have time to turn and flip him the bird, he could hear Blake calling his name down the hallway. He glanced around the finished basement, thankful when he found a neatly folded stack of sweats on a shelf. He jumped across the room, grabbing a pair of pants and pulling them on moments before Blake came around the corner.

"There you are." She stopped, and her eyebrows pulled down into an adorable frown. "You work out barefoot? That can't be safe."

"I showered." He stepped forward and put his hands on her shoulders. "I was coming to look for you. Jasper told me what happened. Are you all right?"

"I'm okay." She leaned down and rested her forehead against his bare chest. "Is Jasper okay? You didn't murder him and hide his body in a closet, did you?"

Riley rubbed her back, loving the feel of her in his arms. "No." He smirked to himself. "I punched him though. I couldn't help it."

She pulled back, her bottom lip between her teeth. "It was so weird, the whole thing. Like, we were fine and we were having fun. We had a good talk. Then all of a sudden I started to feel so flushed. He was worried about me, then he turned on a dime and got all creepy. Then he sniffed me and licked me." She sighed. "You'd think after the other stuff I let him do to me, a simple lic—"

"Nope." Riley placed his fingers over her mouth, stopping her from saying anything more. He couldn't hear her talk about Jasper like that. He couldn't know she thought about the way Jasper touched her at the cabin. "Tell me more about how you were feeling? Flushed?"

She nipped at his pinkie before he could remove it all the way. "I got hot, like blood-boiling hot. It came out of nowhere basically."

"Basically?"

She smirked, her eyes dancing, letting Riley know that she was about to say something entirely Blake. "We were coming down the mountain and I was having these flashbacks of us that night—"

"Nope." Riley put his hand over her mouth again, and growled, "I can't hear about you and Jasper."

She swallowed, pulling back her head. "Not Jasper, *you*. I was remembering you from that night. The way everything went down, and the way you made me feel. Then boom. It was like I walked into an incinerator."

Riley couldn't help his grin. His girl, his mate, was thrown into a frenzy by the memory of his touch.

Blake rolled her eyes. "Okay, how smug can one dude look?" She pushed at his chest. "I feel better now though. Oh, and I met a dog?"

"A dog?" Riley had internally cringed every time Blake had called him a dog while he was in wolf form. He didn't love Jace calling him a pussy either. "In the woods?"

"Yeah. He came out of nowhere, putting himself between me and Jasper." She was more animated, talking with her hands. "He was huge and this pretty rust color. He saved me, then helped me back down the mountain. He's super into me." She smiled. Her eyes full of light once again.

"I'm sure he is." Riley couldn't help but mirror her grin, even though he knew he shouldn't encourage her when it came to keeping his wolf secret.

"He's out back with Jace and Axie. They said he could stay in the backyard. I told him I'd sneak him into the house later and he can sleep with us. You want to come meet him?"

"I'm allergic to dogs." Riley threw that out there, hoping it would fix the issue of him and the dog being in the same place at the same time. When had his life turned into a sitcom episode?

"You are? I didn't know that." Blake stuck out her bottom lip, like his admission bummed her out.

"He's a wolf, not a dog, so he's probably already back hanging in the woods."

Her forehead wrinkled. "How did you know that? How does everyone in this house know the difference between a giant-ass dog and a wolf?"

"The woods around here are full of them." Riley gestured behind him to the window Jace had shoved him through.

"Well, I'm going to put some water out for him anyway, in case he decides to stick around." She spun on her heel, pausing on her way out the door. "You want to watch a movie or something? I need to shower Jasper's spit off my neck, but after?"

Riley ground his molars, his hands fisting behind his back where she wouldn't notice. The mere mention of Jasper's tongue on her, and he was thrown back into his jealousy, and his anger spiked.

Jasper had touched her. He'd tried to mark her. If Riley hadn't gotten there in time, Blake would have been hurt, no doubt about it. It was easy to smile while she was standing in front of him safe and happy. If Axie hadn't dragged him to Pen's house, if she hadn't shed light on what was happening between him and Blake... The afternoon would have ended differently. Riley tried to shove those thoughts away. He didn't want to wonder if Jasper would've stopped, he didn't want to picture Blake having to fight him off.

"Yeah, doll face, of course." He joined her at the door, putting his arm around her shoulders and kissing the top of her head. "I need to talk to Jace first, and then I'll come find you." They parted ways at the end of the hallway, and Riley waited until Blake was upstairs before he stomped into the living room.

He reached out and popped Jasper on the back of the head. "Come on, jackoff, your twin wants to see us in his office."

Silently, Jasper followed Riley down the hallway. Jace was already waiting for them, standing behind his glass desk. As soon as they stepped into the room and the door was closed, Riley threw a punch right into Jasper's face. His head whipped to the side, but he didn't go down, which was a testament to how Riley was taking it easy on him.

"Yeah, I deserved that."

"You sure fucking did." Riley glanced down at his fist, making sure he hadn't broken his skin on Jasper's stupid, smug mouth. "I told Blake I punched you when you told me what happened. So now there's proof."

"I'm so fucking sorry, man. Obviously I had no fucking clue what was going to happen when I took her on that hike. You have to see that." Jasper wiped at his lips, using the edge of his shirt to stop the bleeding.

Riley was pissed they'd been alone together in the first place and was irritated neither one of them thought to tell him where they were headed. It was suspish, and made him feel like they were going behind his back. His wolf fucking hated it. "Why in the hell were you taking her on a hike up the mountain by yourself anyway? What was that even about?"

"It was about you." Jasper plopped down into one of the two leather chairs in front of Jace's desk. "We're all going to be in Greenly together. We both refuse to give you up. We needed to find our footing. We needed to learn how to be friends."

Riley softened, marginally, at the honesty in Jasper's tone. He believed his intentions were in the right place, he did. That didn't make any of this okay.

"I knew some shit was going to happen, this is why I didn't want to share—"

"You knew she was yours, really?" Jasper interrupted him, his eyebrows rising with his volume. "Then why in the fuck *did* you agree to share her with me?"

"I mean, no, I didn't know she was *mine*. Not then. I just knew it was a bad fucking idea." Riley would've tried to kill Jasper on the spot if he'd thought for even a moment Blake was his forever. "I didn't realize she was mine until after Axie made me talk to Pen this morning. My anger, my jealousy, it's directed at you, and it has been since we got back to the compound. I was fine the morning after the cabin, but then having her here, knowing you'd touched her. Fuck, man. It was taking everything I had not to beat your ass."

Jasper's tone quieted, his position relaxing out of defense mode. "What did Pen say?"

"At UNC, I'm more human than wolf. I don't run there, I don't shift. My instincts to claim Blake, to recognize what she was to me, were weak. Diluted." Riley sat down in the other chair, the anger leaking out of his body. "Once we got home, and started shifting, I was around my pack—"

Jace spoke up from his spot behind his desk. "Your wolf perked up and started going crazy."

Riley nodded. "I swear, I didn't know."

"Like I didn't know her body was going to completely spaz the fuck out," Jasper added.

"Look. What's done is done." Jace stepped around his desk, his arms crossing over his chest. "No one knew you two fucknuts were going to defile my safe house with your antics. No one knew Blake was meant to be Riley's. No one knew that she was going to follow your ass up that mountain and have her first bonding hot flash and set off your horndog ass." Riley glanced at Jasper and caught him wincing at Jace's words. "But now we do, so we need to figure out where the hell to go from here."

Jace pointed a finger in his direction. "Riley, I know you never wanted to tell Blake about this part of your life. I know that was your plan. That plan is bullshit now, so you need to figure out how to tell your mate what the rest of her life is going to look like." He shifted his focus to his twin. "Jasper, you need to stay the fuck away from her because we all know that you won't be able to handle yourself the next time her body reacts like that. I'm not about to have you and Riley going at it and breaking everything in my house."

Tell your mate what the rest of her life is going to look like? Easier fucking said than done, that was for sure. How did he even begin that conversation? He also felt bad for Jasper, who was basically going to be sentenced to his room until Riley could complete the bond with Blake. Everything was so monumentally fucked up.

Jace cleared his throat, bringing Riley out of his thoughts. "Constantine's still close. He's still watching. He's been on to us for months, and we had no idea. More pictures come every day." He sighed, the sound betraying his exhaustion. "We're stuck in this house for a while longer. I'm not letting anyone leave until I know for sure the threat has been eliminated." Jace stood, his spine straightening and his chin lifting, beta mode activated. "Riley, figure your shit out, talk to Blake. Jasper, stay the hell away from her." He pointed to the door, letting them know that he wanted both orders carried out immediately.

Chapter Twenty-Eight

Riley

Riley fell back onto the bed in his room, the same room he'd stayed in every time he was at Jace and Axie's compound. It had an attached bathroom, skylights that let him watch the snowfall, and a closet he could never fill in a million years. His meeting with their pack beta and Jasper had left a pit in his stomach. There wasn't much time between realizing Blake was his forever and him shifting on a dime to go rescue her from his packmate on that mountain. Since he shifted back though? Things had begun to move faster. Riley understood the powder-keg situation an unbonded pair was, but he was *not* ready to implode Blake's happy little world. She lived for parties and 90s movie sleepovers. The only stress she liked was over where to order takeout from. She was carefree and quick to laugh. Jace expected Riley to walk into her room and tell her magic was real, shifters existed, and she was meant to be bound to him for the rest of her life.

Whether Riley was ready didn't matter. Blake's body was responding to the bond. It was only a matter of time before the hot flashes got someone hurt, or even worse, her symptoms escalated to the pain Molly and Keller experienced. Baze and Pen, too.

He threw his arm over his eyes, trying to organize all his racing thoughts, and took a deep breath, thinking about Blake and how he felt about her. She made him smile. She made him live and have fun. He enjoyed every second he was with her. He loved how much she liked to wear his clothes and eat greasy hamburgers. She was kind, and she never met a stranger. If he was to be tied to one female for the rest of forever, he couldn't do better than Blake, that was for fucking sure. As annoying as having his choices taken away from him were, he had to concede the universe knew what it was doing.

"There you are, sourpuss." Blake came bouncing into his room, leaping into the air and landing beside him on the bed. "Ready for that movie?" She started ticking off titles on her fingers. "*Speed, Broken Arrow, Congo*—"

"*Congo*?" Riley snorted out a laugh. "The one about the giant man-eating gorillas? Is that really considered an action flick?"

"We're running out of nineties action. We might have to mosey on over to killer animals and natural disasters." She rolled to her side, facing him with a wide grin on her beautiful, makeup-free face. Riley loved this version of Blake. Comfy clothes and bare skin. The way she looked at the end of the day, ready to cuddle up next to him. "The nineties have *tons* of those. *Volcano, Dante's Peak, Twister, Deep Blue Sea, Jurassic Park, The River Wild*, which isn't necessarily a natural disaster but there's a raging river and—"

"Speaking of natural disasters." Riley cut off her deflecting movie rant. "We need to talk about what happened with Jasper on that mountain, and what happened to you." The connection between them wasn't a disaster, but Blake's reaction to the things he needed to tell her might very well be.

She wrinkled her nose. "Do we have to?" She reached over his head, grabbing the remote from his nightstand and flooding his nose with her sweet scent. "I was thinking instead we'd watch movies and you'd let me completely avoid the whole thing." She queued up the movie app, logging in with Riley's password. "It's over. Jasper apologized. A dog helped me back down the mountain. We all survived."

"First of all, it was a *wolf*." Riley would never be okay with the dog downgrade. "Second, Jasper touched you when you didn't want him to." He knew Jasper would never intentionally hurt Blake, but what he did was still a violation. Typically, she avoided heavy conversations at all costs, but Riley couldn't let her blow this off. Not when it was only going to keep happening, and not when there was so much she didn't know. "Not to mention, the way you felt."

"I was dehydrated. Altitude sickness." Blake selected *Congo*. "Now, let's watch this epically ridiculous movie about gorillas and the geodes they protect."

Riley sighed, wrapping his arm around her when she settled against his chest. It'd been a long-as-hell day for both of them. One movie wouldn't hurt. Ninety minutes of complete avoidance sounded really fucking fantastic, actually. Hell, he was about to commandeer the rest of her life, he could give her one movie where everything was right in her world.

***

Riley woke alone. The movie was as 90s as he remembered, and he could barely keep his eyes open. At one point he'd seen Blake start to nod off as well, so he thought it'd been safe to close his eyes for a minute. He didn't think she'd leave the room. He sat up, trying to shake off the sleep, which still had hold of his mind. He knew he needed to go find her, needed to lock her in here with him and make her listen. It wasn't safe for her to be wandering around the house with Jasper being here. Riley got to his feet and made it to the door before he heard the sound of shattering glass and Jace yelling his name.

He bolted down the stairs, whipping around the landing and darting toward the open patio doors. Jace had Jasper pinned to the deck and Blake was holding snow in her hands against her cheeks. Fuck. Jace glared daggers at him as he stepped out into the chaos. "Something you forgot to do, dickhead?"

Jasper wasn't struggling, and Riley couldn't determine whether Blake's episode was over or Jace was being super beta. Either way, he was in deep shit. He'd told Jace he'd talk to Blake, that he wouldn't let things reach an explosive level. Yet, there was glass all over the deck and Jasper had blood dripping down his closed fist.

"I didn't know she left."

"No." Jace pointed an accusing finger in his direction. "You were supposed to find her and tell her."

"Tell me what?" Blake pulled her hands away from her face, her expression confused. "Why is Jasper bleeding?" She got to her feet, dusting the snow off her leggings and not really cleaning them off. "Why am I out here?" She looked across the patio to Riley. "Am I losing my mind? Do I have split personalities or something? I need to be committed, don't I? That's it, I've gone crazy and no one wants to tell me. I need to go to one of those uber-creepy mental institutions and—"

"For fuck's sake, Riley," Jace growled. "Get her out of here. And don't let her leave your goddamn room until she knows everything."

Riley hoisted a still-rambling Blake over his shoulder, carrying her back inside the house, careful to avoid all the broken glass on the way.

Jace was pissed. Jasper was probably feeling guilty for his inability to control his shifter, and Blake was convinced that she had slowly lost her grip on reality. This was the day from hell that refused to fucking end.

"Hey, what happened?" Axie came from her bedroom, pausing in the living room with her gaze darting from the back deck and Riley heading toward the stairs with Blake in his arms. "Did you tell her?"

"No," Riley gritted out.

"It's split personalities, isn't it? I'm like Ed Norton in *Fight Club*." Blake went limp over his shoulder, her hands brushing against his ass as he started up the stairs.

"You know you picked Corey's clone, right?"

He paused at Axie's barely contained humor. Glancing behind him, he asked, "What?"

"She relates serious situations to movies." She was ticking points off on her black-tipped nails. "But she's hilarious, she loves to bust people's balls, she's dramatic...hell, she even has a dude's name." Axie's eyes danced with amusement. "You two are going to be fine, Riley. I promise."

Chapter Twenty-Nine

Blake

Riley dumped Blake on the bed, standing before her with his hands on his hips. He was gorgeous, in a wholesome way she found increasingly enticing. When she woke up pressed to his side, she had a huge urge to climb on top of him and have her wicked way. Those thoughts had been creeping into her mind more and more, ever since the cabin. Ugh. The cabin. She constantly had flashbacks of her night with Jasper and Riley. She dreamt of them. The way she felt being passed back and forth, the way they played with her body. So fucking perfect.

"What are you thinking about? Stop it." Riley was glaring down at her, his green eyes narrowed. "Your face is getting all flushed."

She bit her lips together, trying to switch her focus onto something like baseball. It seemed to work with guys and unwanted boners, at least in movies. Baseball. Riley played baseball. She bet he looked hella handsome in his uniform, those tight pants hugging his ass.

"Blake," Riley snapped. "You're getting overheated."

She met his gaze. "How can you tell?"

He swallowed thickly, his hands dropping. "I can see the blush on your face, and I can smell the change in you." He dropped on the mattress beside her, looking utterly exhausted.

"You can smell me?" She was confused, but that wasn't new. She'd been confused for days now. She'd hooked up with her best friend, and his best friend. She was flown to Haxton on a private plane to be locked away in a compound with people she'd never met because of some threat she didn't quite understand. She sort of lost her shit on a mountain, Jasper sniffed and licked her, and then she was saved by a dog. As of a few minutes ago, she discovered she was developing multiple personalities.

It'd been a fucking rough winter break.

"We need to talk, doll face." Riley reached for her hands, threading their fingers together and pulling her up until she was sitting facing him. "You're not crazy, and you don't have split personalities."

"That's a relief." She cracked a smile when he snorted out a chuckle. He looked so serious, so down, but she was happy she could still make him laugh. Her sourpuss needed her in his life. She'd known that since the first moment she'd laid eyes on him. "The dog was real, right? I didn't make him up?"

"It's a wolf." He shook his head, like he was daring her to call it a dog one more time. "And yes, it was real. You saw it, and so did Jace and Axie, right?" She nodded. "See? Real. I told you, you aren't crazy."

"Then what am I?" Blake sighed, letting the weight of everything she'd been ignoring come to the surface. "Because nothing is making sense."

His gaze searched hers, his fingers tightening, intertwined with hers. Blake's stomach twisted, almost afraid of his answer. "You're my mate."

"Come again?" Blake couldn't have heard him right. There was no way *mate* came out of her best friend's mouth. "Like your mate? Like the Australian word for buddy?"

"Everything I'm about to tell you, um, uh, it's going to be hard to understand. I need you to listen, okay? I need you to keep an open mind, and I need you to not freak out and leave this room. It's not safe for you downstairs, not right now." He shook her hands lightly. "Promise me you won't leave this room."

None of this was helping her believe she wasn't actually losing her mind. Blake looked past Riley to the closed bedroom door. Bolting never crossed her mind. As weird as all this was, she knew that leaving him wasn't something she'd want to do. Crazy or not, he was her ride or die. "I promise."

"Okay. Uh." Riley got to his feet, pacing at the foot of the bed and shaking out his hands. She looked down at her own, and felt the loss of his touch, something she'd never noticed before. "I'm a shifter. I, well, *we* are a pack of shifters. Which are real, by the way, wolf shifters at least. And we mate for life. Axie isn't Jace's fiancée, she's his mate. The universe, it creates a perfect match for each of us, and when we find that match, we're compelled to complete the bond. To claim them. To mate. That's what's happening with you," he motioned between them, "with us. You're mine and since we haven't finished the bond, your body is sort of spazzing out. The hot flashes, that's your body seeking mine out. The wolf who saved you, that was me."

"You're the dog?" After all the things that spilled from her best friend's mouth over the last few minutes, she wasn't sure why that one was what stuck out the most.

"I'm the *wolf*." Riley all but growled at her misuse of the term *dog*, which made more sense now.

"You're the wolf." She snorted out a laugh, although nothing was particularly funny. "I wanted to keep you. I wanted to get you a collar and take you back to Greenly. I wanted to sneak you into the house and let you sleep on my bed."

"Yeah."

"Jace said you couldn't come inside because you had fleas." Her giggles took over, making her fall back on the bed. "He said you were small, and you pissed on his boots."

"Blake, doll, come on." He grabbed her hands and pulled back to sitting. "The manic giggles are starting to freak me out."

"Manic." She nodded, covering her mouth to try to regain control. "My best friend is a wolf, and he belongs to a pack."

"All the males you met shift. Females don't shift, they don't carry the gene. But all the males, they shift. We're all wolves."

"Jasper?"

Riley joined her on the bed again. "Jasper is a shifter, yes. The reason he sniffed and licked you, the reason he's been acting so strange, is because he isn't bonded. He doesn't have a mate. His wolf can sense the change in your body when you get overheated, when you're seeking out the bond. It's enticing, and it's hard for him to stay away."

"You have mates, real mates, for life." She seemed to be having a mild case of out-of-body experience. It was as if she was watching the conversation unfold from a distance. She knew she was the one asking these questions, that this was real and this was happening to her. She felt removed though. She wasn't scared, she wasn't thinking about running out the door. She should be, but she wasn't, and that made everything even more surreal.

"Corey, Molly, Madden, Pen, and Axie. They're all mated to their partners. It's like being married, but at a molecular level. They were made for each other, destined from the start."

"I'm your mate?" She swallowed past the lump in her throat. Why wasn't she freaking out? She lived for overly dramatic reactions, and yet she was taking all this craziness in stride. "Are you compelling me right now? Is that what this is? Some *Vampire Diaries* situation where you've compelled me to stay calm? Oh my god. Are vampires real too?"

Riley smiled, his grin taking over his face. "There's my girl." He chuckled, reaching for her hand again. "You had me worried there for a minute." He kissed her palms, something he'd done a couple times since the cabin, something that made her insides ignite. "Vampires aren't real, that I know of anyway. I'm not compelling you. We don't possess that ability. You were created for me, made to be mine. You aren't freaking out because this is the way it was always meant to be."

She thought back to the first moment she'd seen Riley. It wasn't when she busted into his dorm room as she'd let him believe. It was an hour before when she'd watch him walk the hall, his head down and a frown on his handsome face. Her heart ached for him, and she'd instantly wanted to make him smile. So she'd taken note of which room he'd entered, and she'd made a point to meet him. She'd been drawn to him before she even met him. She'd wanted to know him.

"Are we mated? The universe wills it, so it is?"

Riley shook his head. "No, we haven't finished the bonding process. We started it, accidentally, which is why your body is spazzing out on us. It wants us to finish it."

"When did we start it?" Blake couldn't remember anything out of the ordinary happening, some accidental voodoo-like ceremony, which got interrupted by their Postmates order.

"The cabin."

She couldn't help her gasp. "Oh my god. Am I mated to Jasper too? I'm going to have two mates?"

"No." His voice had dropped several octaves. He was growling more than talking. "You are not mated to Jasper, you aren't his. Ever." He took a deep breath, like he was trying to calm himself down. "I didn't know then that you were meant for me. Obviously. If I had, then I would have never—"

"Shared me with your best friend."

"Please, don't talk about that right now." He was speaking through clenched teeth, his grip on her hands tightening. "It's really hard for me to swallow the fact that my best friend has been with my mate."

"That's why you and Jasper seem so weird, so tense?" She waited for him to nod before continuing. "Is sex the process? The way to complete the bond between us?" He nodded again. "We already did that though." She did that with him *and* Jasper, but apparently that topic made him want to rail on his "packmate."

"We used condoms." Riley nodded at her shocked expression. "There has to be nothing between us, no barriers."

"Good thing I'm on the pill." Blake twisted her lips to one side, images running rampant in her mind. "I don't know about you, but I am not ready to have a litter of wolf pups running around my dorm room."

"We'll have human babies." Riley rolled his eyes, which made her happy. They were still them. Still friends. Still able to joke and make each other laugh. "Are you saying you're okay with all this? You're not going to sneak out in the middle of the night and disappear into the mountains?"

None of the last few weeks had been normal, but learning magical creatures existed somehow made it all seem a little less crazy. Which was pure insanity in and of itself. She was only nineteen. She had her whole adult life ahead of her. She'd never planned to settle down with one person until she'd seen the world, experienced everything imaginable. She wanted a career and independence before she picked one dick to grow old and wrinkly with. She knew she should be freaking out, should be firing off questions and looking for a loophole. Searching desperately for more time, a way out.

She wasn't. She felt calm. She felt at peace, safe. She'd been drawn to Riley instantly, and always. He made her happy. He made her laugh. He accepted her, every part of her. She'd never felt as cherished as she did with him, as special. He was the best friend she'd ever had, and she couldn't imagine her life without him in it.

Since the cabin, she'd been drawn to him in a way she hadn't been before. She craved his touch, and she wanted to be surrounded by his scent all the time. The memory of them together, the way he felt inside her, the way he kissed, the way his teeth felt against her flesh...

"You better be thinking of only me only right now. I swear I'll rip out his throat."

"How can you always tell?" She should be embarrassed he kept catching her thinking about him naked, but there never really was much shame in her game.

"Your body heats up, and your smell changes. It gets sweeter." Riley leaned forward, running his nose up the column of her throat and sending chills racing down her back. "You're mine. I'll always be able to tell, doll face."

She hummed, wanting to pull him closer. "The feminist in me should really hate you saying *I'm yours*."

"I'm yours too." He kissed her collarbone, steadily erasing the line defining their friendship. Since they'd had kinky threesome sex, the line was really more like a rubber band at this point. "I belong to you as much as you belong to me. I'll spend the rest of my life living only for you."

Chapter Thirty

Riley

Riley kissed her again, his tongue darting out to taste the flush on her flesh. She was turned on, she wanted more. Her body had been fluctuating back and forth all day. He wondered what would've happened if they hadn't had this talk. Would she have come to him, asked him to touch her? Or would she have pushed those feelings away, afraid of the consequences?

"Jasper keeps getting hurt because of me." She pulled back slightly, looking into his eyes.

He frowned at her softly spoken words. She'd been made to feel uncomfortable. She'd been put in a bad position by his packmate, and yet she felt bad for Jasper, not herself. "Jasper keeps getting hurt because his wolf is a horny dipshit."

"You hit him. You guys are fighting. He was bleeding, pinned down by Jace on the deck." She shook her head, biting at her pink bottom lip. "I don't want to be the reason things are tense here, or strained between you two. I don't want to be the reason Jasper is upset."

"That's not a reason to complete the bond, doll face." Riley tucked a wayward hair behind her ear. "When you make that choice, it needs to be because *you* want it. You want me, you want to be tied to me for the rest of forever."

"My body—"

"Can be controlled." He shook his head, cutting off her argument. "We can manipulate things, keep the hot flashes at bay for a while. As long as you don't start experiencing any pain, we have time."

He'd been terrified to tell her what he was, what he'd dragged her into. Everyone else had been right though. There was nothing to fear with his girl. She was made for him, made for this life, and she'd taken everything he'd told her better than he'd ever expected. She was selfless, hilarious, kind, strong. She was perfect.

"How do we manipulate it? I need to walk around with snow in my pants?" She wrinkled her nose at her own suggestion. "Maybe an ice pack. The snow would start to melt and make a mess. I could drink cold beer all day, that sounds like a fun way to finish out this lockdown."

"I need to make you come."

Her eyebrows shot to her hairline. "Are you being serious?"

He shrugged, chuckling at her expression. "I guess you could make yourself come. The guys always made it sound like it needed to be them, but maybe that was their dicks talking. I could call Pen and ask if it's mate specific, or if—"

"You can do it." She cut him off, a wicked smile on her face. "I mean, why do it myself when I have a hot mate on standby to make me scream? You said it yourself, I'm not crazy."

"You're sure?" He wanted to touch her. He wanted his mouth on her. He wanted her taste on his tongue, the sound of her whimpers filling his ears. It was as if finding out that she was meant for him had given his body permission to *want* her. To desire her. He'd always thought she was beautiful, but now he found her utterly irresistible.

She nodded, her bottom lip between her straight white teeth. "Yes."

"Come here." He gestured her closer, his hands going to her hips as she climbed into his lap. His palm rested against her neck, her pulse rapid against his fingers. He pulled her closer, kissing her lips, humming in appreciation.

He threaded his hand in her blonde hair, dragging her head back and giving him better access to her slender throat. He nipped, sucked, and licked his way down to her breast.

Taking off her shirt to give him full access to her sweet flesh. She whimpered when he took her nipples into his mouth, tugging on them the way he remembered she liked.

He moved over her, pushing her back onto the mattress before dragging her pants down her toned legs. She was gorgeous, lying under him in nothing but a pair of hot pink panties. He put his palm on her chest, dancing his fingertips down her body until they reached the edge of the lace. He moved forward and used his teeth to drag the fabric away from her.

She was writhing on the bed, her hand in his hair, urging him to go where she wanted him.

He closed his mouth over her clit, flicking at her with his tongue. He pushed her thighs down to the bed, baring her to him completely. She whispered his name as he slid two fingers inside her heat.

She was so close already, so close to the edge. Her body was craving his, craving the unfinished bond between them. She came apart moments later, her moans growing louder, more frantic. He refused to let up, and sucked on her through it, building a new orgasm almost instantly.

He planned to make her come again and again.

All night, in fact, having her the only way he'd let himself.

Chapter Thirty-One

Blake

The sun woke her. It always seemed to shine so much brighter after a good snowfall. Like the universe wanted to show off its beauty with a spotlight. Speaking of the universe: Riley shifted into a wolf, and she was made to be his mate for the rest of her life. She rolled over, facing the ceiling, her head resting on his shoulder. Their conversation last night was a lot to take in, and completely normal at the same time. It was as if they were discussing the weather when in reality they were speaking about a tornado about to touch down and change their landscape forever.

What came after that talk was nice. Better than nice, it was fantastic. Riley had made her come, over and over again. He couldn't seem to get enough of her body, her kisses and her cries. Every time she'd come down, catch her breath, he'd amp her up again. She definitely wasn't complaining. If that was what it took to keep her body in check, she was *all* for it.

They'd gone from friends to so much more in the matter of one evening. She supposed that was the way it always went though, right? One minute you were living your life, drinking, partying, having threesomes. Then bam. The universe hit you upside the head with your person. Tons of people married their best friend. Her new shifter life wasn't really all that different. Other than the supernatural magic that made her boyfriend turn into an actual wolf.

"Let me guess, you're starving, hungrier than you've ever been in your entire life, and you need food and coffee before you simply perish?"

She laughed lightly, rolling onto her stomach to meet his smiling eyes. "Don't take my lines, sourpuss." She kissed his lips, because she wanted to, because she could. "Am I allowed to go downstairs? Will Jasper be okay?"

"As long as you pay attention to how you're feeling, pay attention to your body, you should be able to sense when you need to come lock yourself up here." He grabbed her face in his hands. "But you've got to stop worrying about Jasper, okay? Your safety is what's important to me. You are what's important."

She knew he wanted her to be selfish in this, to think of herself and not worry about anyone's feelings but her own. That wasn't possible though. She cared for Jasper, and she hated being the reason that things weren't copasetic between them. She didn't know if it was because she'd been intimate with him, or that he was an extension of Riley's family. Either way, she cared. Jasper mattered.

She nodded. "If I get horny, I come lock myself in this room and text you to come make it better. Got it." She winked. "So far, on my way to mated is nothing but perks. I don't know why you were so nervous to tell me."

He got out of bed, dragging her along with him. "Come on, doll, let's make you scream my name one more time in the shower, for good measure."

***

Blake and Riley stepped into the living room, holding hands and looking thoroughly coupled up. Axie was on Jace's lap, a cup of coffee to her lips. Jasper stretched out on the couch, his cell held up above his face. She felt mildly embarrassed facing everyone. They'd all known about what was happening before she did. She'd been the reason for the mess yesterday, for Jasper getting punched, for whoever had been bleeding while she used the snow to cool herself off. They were a family, and she was the newbie. She wanted to be accepted, she wanted to fit into Riley's life here in Haxton the way she did back in Greenly.

"Since you're both down here, I'm assuming you talked." Jace peeked around Axie's shoulders to send a glare Riley's way. "If not, then take your asses back up those stairs."

Riley pulled her into the living room, setting her down in an empty armchair. "We talked. Calm your beta ass." *Beta?* Like as in alpha and beta, like as in actual wolf behavior? They'd talked, true, but apparently there was a lot more she needed to learn about her new life. "I'll go get you some breakfast." Riley dipped down and placed a kiss on the top of her head before moving toward the kitchen.

She was left alone with his pack, with his best friend. The best friend who'd seen her incredibly naked and licked her neck yesterday. When she left home for college, she vowed to live life to the fullest. She didn't know how much more she could handle at this point.

"You, uh, feeling okay?" Jasper sat up, moving farther away from her against the opposite arm of the couch.

She understood his hesitation, but she hated that he felt uncomfortable around her. A lot had changed in the last couple of weeks, but she, Riley, and Jasper would be living and spending time together at UNC. There couldn't be this awkwardness between them.

"Jasper, do you think we could talk?" She glanced behind her to the double glass patio doors. "Maybe outside? For just a minute?" She could see the reluctance on his face. "I feel fine, I promise. I know what to watch out for now. Riley explained it all." Not to mention he'd made her come so many times over the last twelve hours she'd lost count.

Jasper's gaze moved to Jace for a moment before he nodded, got to his feet, and opened the doors. The cold air seeped in almost instantly, making Blake wished she'd have put on a few more layers. She followed Jasper outside, not going too far from the door. She wanted to be within eyesight of Jace and Axie, to make them all feel safer.

"I wanted to apologize for yester—"

"No." Jasper shook his head, cutting her off. "There is nothing for you to apologize for. I should be the one telling you how sorry I am. I can't always control my wolf, and I fucking hate it. I hate I've done these things to Maddi, Axie, and now you. Shit. Blake. I need you to know that I would never hurt you, never on purpose."

She could feel his anguish. His tone and his explanation screamed it. He looked stricken, distraught he could've hurt her. She didn't know the first thing about how he was feeling, about the things he dealt with as a shifter. She knew he was a good guy though. She believed he would never intentionally hurt her.

"There's always been someone there to stop me, to pull me away." His voice cracked, and her heart ached for him. "I have to believe my wolf would never let things go too far...that I'd be able to stop myself."

"Jasper." Blake reached out and put her hand on his shoulder, wanting to help him. It was clear that he was beating himself up, struggling with who he was. Who his wolf was. She didn't want to be the reason that he was feeling so low, so uncertain of himself.

"Everything okay?" Riley stuck his head out the door, his gaze moving between the two of them, his muscles tight.

There was no problem, and there wouldn't be another one if she could help it. She refused to be the reason there was tension between Riley and his best friend. They were packmates, brothers. Close as hell. They even shared chicks. Although she supposed that was over now too, because of her, again. She wouldn't be the reason Jasper was hurting either.

"Everything is fine." She moved her hand to cup Jasper's cheek, ignoring the low growl coming from Riley. "Right? We're all going to be fine, besties for life."

Jasper laughed, the tension finally leaving his face. "Besties for life." Jasper slung his arm around her shoulders, then Riley's too. leading them back into the warmth of the living room. "Roommates, besties, pack, family. All the things."

Blake collapsed on the couch where Axie was sitting, Jace nowhere in sight. "All the things for sure." She smirked at Axie, winking before adding, "I doubt another dude is as close with their packmate's girl as you are, right?"

Riley growled her name and Jasper threw his head back, laughing. "Life is going to be interesting with you, doll face."

Axie lay down with her head in Blake's lap. "I, for one, am glad when Jasper leaves the nest he's still going to have someone who can keep up with his sarcastic fuckboy ass." She grinned over at Riley's still-frowning face. "You picked a good one, Rye."

Chapter Thirty-Two

Riley

Blake *was* a good one, no doubt about it. He wasn't sure he picked her though. She'd picked him, and the universe had agreed. Fate was smarter than him, and for that he was eternally grateful. Riley knew Blake wanted to talk to Jasper alone, and he'd been okay with it in theory. Seeing the two of them on the porch together had been harder to handle than he'd thought. He knew a lot his discomfort had to do with the bond being incomplete. He'd seen his coaches go through it. Jace too. Once he and Blake were fully mated, he'd become a lot less aggressive and jealous. Until she got pregnant, then it would all return full force. In his experience, life mated to a shifter wasn't always easy, but it was always beautiful.

"Jasper and I need to go talk with Jace. You going to be okay?" Riley rested his hands on Blake's shoulders, smiling when she leaned her head back for a kiss.

"Unless Axie is going to try to dry hump me, I think I'll be fine."

She spoke against his lips, making him want to drag her back upstairs to bed. Now that he knew she was his, he couldn't get enough. He wanted more than anything to complete the claiming, for them to be fully bonded. He'd never push her into something she wasn't ready for though. They had the rest of their lives to fuck like bunnies. He was looking forward to it.

Axie giggled, smirking wickedly. "You never know with me."

"If you two are going to get it on, I think I'll stay here in the living room." Jasper made a move to sit back down.

Riley grabbed him by the back of the shirt, hoisting him to his feet and dragging him down the hall. He knew Blake was feeling fine. He could tell when her body started to react to the bond. That didn't mean he was okay leaving her alone with Jasper though.

Jace shut the door behind them, waiting until they both sat before he rounded the desk and took up his beta power stance before them. "How'd it go last night?"

"Since your bedroom is downstairs," Jasper chuckled, "let me give you a recap of the sounds I heard floating up."

"It went fine." Riley punched Jasper in the arm. "She took everything in stride, like you said she would. She understands what's happening with her body, and she knows what signs to look for and how to manipulate it. I can tell too, if I'm close enough to her. There shouldn't be any more problems."

"What about completing the bond? That's the only sure way to keep all three of you safe once you get back to Greenly." Jace crossed his arms over his chest. "We're leaking the info on Constantine tomorrow, then it's only a matter of time before he's behind bars and the three of you are out of here. You can be next to her constantly while you're locked in the house, but what happens when you're on campus? You have different schedules. You can't be with her nonstop."

"You guys don't even live in the same building." Jasper shifted in his seat, rubbing at the faded bruise under his eye. "What happens if I run into her first, man? I hate this. I hate that I have the potential to hurt her, to hurt you."

Riley could feel the desperation coming from his packmate, and it tore at his heart. Blake was the most important person here. She was his everything. That didn't mean Jasper ceased to exist for him.

"She said she was ready, but I needed her to take a day or two and let everything sink in." Riley loved how selfless Blake was ready to be to save Jasper any more torment. In this though, she needed to be selfish, she needed time. This was the rest of her life they were talking about. Riley had understood the concept of mates since he was five. Blake, on the other hand, had learned about shifters' existence less than twenty-four hours ago. "Blake doesn't want Jasper to suffer, and she doesn't want to come between us." Riley pointed at Jasper, with a death glare. "If you make one goddamn joke about her coming between us, I'll rip out your tongue."

Jasper held his hands up, smirking. "I wasn't going to, I swear." He pursed his lips. "I thought it though, not gonna lie."

"For fuck's sake." Jace scrubbed his hands down his face. "How the hell are you three going to live together with this huge thing between you? You both hooked up with her, at the same time. Your wolf is never going to forget that." He was looking at Riley, fear for his twin etched in his face. "You going to wake up one day, remember he tag-teamed your girl and then murder my brother?"

Riley had lain awake last night, thinking about Jasper, thinking about how angry he'd been at him. Riley was jealous, he was irritated. He didn't like that Jasper had been intimate with his mate. It wasn't how things worked in their world. Mates weren't meant to be shared sexually. It went against every instinct their wolves had. Blake was *his* girl. She belonged to him and his wolf. They would protect her with their life. They would cherish every inch of her for eternity. But sharing? Never again.

"On some level, my wolf knew Blake was mine, right? My wolf may have been dormant, but he still existed inside me. He was closer to the surface that night in the cabin. I could feel him. And yet we, he and I, still let it happen. I wasn't angry with Jasper in the moment, and not the next morning either. I wasn't really mad at him until we got back to the compound. I didn't want to rip his head off until Blake got here either." Riley looked at Jasper, taking in the pained expression on his face, the regret at what his boredom in that cabin had caused. "I don't think my wolf minded sharing her that one time. It's like I'm not mad about the cabin. Now that's she almost mine, I'm angry he has the *memory* of that night, I'm pissed the fuck off she still thinks about it. I don't know. I don't think I'm explaining it well."

"I get it." For once there was no playfulness in Jasper's tone, no joking or sarcasm. "It was an ending and a beginning. It was the closure we both needed. I needed to be there, to bear witness."

Riley nodded, knowing Jasper had put how he felt into perfect words when he'd been unable to.

"I will never understand the two of you." Jace shook his head. "I literally want to track down and kill every dick that ever touched my mate before mine." He wagged a finger between them. "And you two had yours there at the same time."

Riley growled, low and long, not appreciating the way Jace was talking about Blake. It was Jasper who spoke up though. "Don't make things worse, bro."

Jace held his hands up in surrender. "This is your deal. As long as you two don't try to kill each other, I'm staying out of it." He reached behind him and handed them each a flyer. "This place near campus came on the market a couple weeks ago. I bought it."

Riley studied the stone and cedar craftsman-style home. There were three bedrooms, two baths, a detached two-car garage, and a spacious yard, which backed up to dense woods. It was way too nice a house for three college freshmen, and an over-the-top gesture.

"You bought us a house?" Jasper glanced at Riley. "The three of us?"

"I bought an investment property for the three of you to live in until graduation. Yes." Jace crossed his arms again, his signature stance. "You think you can handle it? Then it's yours for as long as you're in school." He pointed Jasper. "Don't trash it. No crazy parties."

"Wow, man, this is too nice, thank you." Riley understood Jace had more money than he knew what to do with. He also knew that Jace recognized a good investment when he saw it, so it wasn't a gift. Which made it a lot easier to accept in Riley's book. "Don't we have to live on campus our freshman year though?"

Jace waved away his concern. "I took care of that already." He pulled two sets of keys out of his pocket, tossing them their way. "You'll have to get Blake a key. I didn't know you'd be mated up before you even moved in. Don't kill each other." With that he all but dismissed them from his office, mumbling about how he had real work to do and was done dealing with their dicks' problems.

Axie and Blake were right where they left them, lying on the couch together. They were both on their phones, showing each other things back and forth, laughing. Blake fit in with his pack so well, as if she'd always been part of them. He loved that she was instantly at ease with Axie. Hell, he even enjoyed her sarcastic back-and-forth with Jasper when he wasn't trying to lick her in the woods.

"I'm bored. Let's have some fun." Jasper plopped down in an armchair, pouting like a petulant child. "I'm tired of being cooped inside this house."

Axie sat up, placing her bare feet on the rug. "Whatever you've got brewing in that thick skull of yours, I'm down."

"Hide-and-seek?" Jasper rubbed his hands together like an evil genius.

"Abso-fucking-lutely not." Jace came into the room, rolling his eyes with an annoyed expression on his face.

"What the hell? I thought you had *real* work to do? Why are you in here, ruining our fun?" Jasper threw his arms into the air dramatically.

"There is a murderous criminal watching our every move. He knows where all the pack lives, and he's threatened every member. He's not low-level. He's proving that over and over." Jace pointed at Blake, then went to the bar cart and poured himself a couple fingers of whiskey. "Your best friend's mate is constantly moments away from throwing off enough heat and pheromones to make you actually insane." He sat on the couch, pulling Axie into his lap, scowling when she stole his drink. "And you want me to let the lot of you run around outside, in the dark? Are you fucking high?"

"Yes." Jasper nodded, a smile on his face.

Riley didn't doubt Jasper was telling the truth. He'd been so on edge and afraid of hurting Blake. It was hard to get too messed up, for too long. The shifter inside them burned off the chemicals too fast, but it would definitely give him a momentary reprieve from all the shit going on inside his head.

"Pick another game." Jace's tone had a finality to it that couldn't be swayed. Riley swore he'd acquired it once he became pack beta. He couldn't remember Jace being able to shut them down so effectively when they were younger.

"What about hide-and-seek *inside* the house?" Jasper sounded hopeful and Axie clapped her hands together in agreement. The two of them were so much alike. Riley knew that once Jasper was out of the house and up in Greenly with him and Blake, Jace's daily life would get a little easier. Axie's on the other hand? She was going to be bored to tears. "We're all safe and locked in, no criminals to snatch us out of the dark."

Jace snorted. "Except Blake is a ticking time bomb."

"I know I shouldn't really be offended by the truth, but still, harsh." Blake pouted out her bottom lip, making Axie giggle.

Riley sat down, pulling Blake's feet into his lap and resting his hands on her shins. "I topped her off before we came downstairs." The way they were together, the casual touches, the familiarity, had been there from day one. He should've seen the truth sooner. He should've paid attention to the feeling of home that overwhelmed him when she was near. "She should be good for a while."

"Is this normal for shifters?" Blake wrinkled her cute nose. "Like do you guys always causally talk about making your girlfriends come?"

Jace choked on the sip of whiskey he'd taken, his gaze cutting to Riley. "You had to go and find someone exactly like those two, didn't you?"

Riley grinned, instantly understanding what Jace was saying, his comment mirroring Riley's thoughts from moments before. Blake was a lot like Axie, and Axie was a lot like Jasper. They were a blunt, hilarious, wicked triad.

"All these guys do tend to be pretty open about the frequency of getting their dicks wet." Axie tapped her chin, contemplating. "They never share details though. Even when you ask for them."

"Can we stop talking about sex things?" Jasper squirmed in his seat. "I'm using my hand until we get back to campus, and I'm feeling pretty fucking bummed about it. Turning me on with dirty talk isn't helping."

Jace reached over and punched his twin in the arm. "Don't fucking say my mate is turning you on." He hit him again. "What the hell is wrong with you?"

"I didn't say *she* was turning me on. I said this conversation is giving me a semi." Jasper rolled his eyes, rubbing at his arm. "Can we play inside hide-and-seek or not?"

Jace sighed. "Fine." He pointed a finger at Riley's face, his eyes narrowed, letting everyone know his asshole beta side was about to come out. "But if something happens down here, you two are grounded to your room until you finish that fucking bond, you understand?"

Riley and Blake both nodded, like children who'd been scolded and warned.

Chapter Thirty-Three

Blake

Hide-and-seek in the house sounded fun, in theory. Jace's warning kind of took the wind out of her sails though. She didn't want to be the reason anyone got hurt. She'd already offered to go ahead with the bond, to finish whatever the universe had created between her and Riley. It was him who was delaying things. He wanted her to be ready, to take her time and make sure she was all in. Riley was a good guy, a great guy. She'd never met someone as genuine and kind as he was. She'd seen that from the first night they'd hung out. The more time they spent together, the more good qualities she found. He was funny, smart, athletic. He was sexy in a cute way that not many dudes would be able to pull off.

Blake felt lucky. She felt grateful. She'd lain awake that morning trying to freak out. She went over the last couple of weeks in her mind, looking for a reason to lose her shit. It was as if her mind refused to spiral. The only feelings she could conjure were contentment. Happiness. Sure, her life was a bit in danger, but she felt completely safe here in the mountains with her mate and his pack. She was made for this life. She knew that with every fiber of her being.

Try as she might to find a pitfall in everything Riley had told her, she was excited. Ready.

"Couples can't hide together." Jasper came back from the kitchen, passing out beers to everyone except Jace, who had his expensive whiskey in his fancy crystal glass. "It's not fair and you'll just end up humping."

Blake glanced to Riley, smiling when he winked. She'd love to do some dry humping in a closet. She'd found Riley attractive from the moment she first saw him, but over the past couple of weeks that feeling had grown into a monster. She *wanted* him every second of every day.

"Fair enough." Axie hopped off Jace's lap. "Who is counting first?"

"I'll be it." Jace propped his feet up on the coffee table, leaning back as he casually sipped his drink.

"Okay, but you have to actually come find us." Axie glared down at him, her hands on her hips. "You can't say you're going to be *it* and then turn on a World War Two documentary and never come find us."

Blake laughed as she sat up, taking a pull from the cold beer in her hand. She could one hundred percent see Jace doing that. Posting up, content to let them stay in their hiding places all night so he could get some peace and quiet. He was like a gorgeous broody old man.

"I'll seek." Jace smirked over the rim of his glass. "But you better hide well, babe, because we both know what'll happen when I find you."

Blake pursed her lips. "Wait. Can't your wolf parts sniff us out? Is that even fair?" She'd never played hide-and-seek with three wolf boys, but she assumed they had an unfair advantage.

"Playground rules, you've gotta use the clothespin. I'll go find one." Jasper left the room, disappearing down the hall Blake knew eventually led to the basement.

"This is all getting more annoying by the second." Jace rolled his eyes. "I don't want to walk around my own home with a clothespin on my nose like I'm fucking ten years old."

No one said anything until Jasper came back, holding the old-school wooden pin out to his brother, a triumphant smile on his face. "Playground rules. You know it's the only fair way."

Jace snatched the contraption out of Jasper's hand. "Go hide before I change my mind and lock all of you in your rooms."

Blake could see why Axie and Jasper liked giving Jace such a hard time. If Riley was a sourpuss, then Jace was a stick-up-his-ass old man. He needed people to remind him life wasn't all doom and gloom and it was okay to laugh and act his real age.

Axie giggled at his threat, then took off across the house the moment he closed his eyes and began counting out loud.

Blake darted into the kitchen, laughing when Riley grabbed her around the waist and started carrying her like a sack of potatoes. "What are you doing? Couples can't hide together." He whipped her around, set her on her feet, and started backing her into the pantry.

"We need to stick together, it's safer for everyone this way." Riley cupped her face in the dark, kissing her until she melted into him. She wanted to go upstairs. She wanted to climb his body. She wanted to demand he claim her. She moaned against his lips, then stumbled as the wall behind her gave way.

Riley caught her before she could go down, pulling her into a dimly lit room. "What is this place? A secret room behind the pantry?" Blake spun in a circle, taking in her new surroundings. There was a small kitchen, a living room setup, and a row of bunk beds against one cinder block wall. "Is this a bunker?"

"It's a safe room." Riley shut the door, the sound of the click echoing loudly in the quiet room.

"Dude, what the fuck?" Riley and Blake both spun around at the sound of Jasper's outrage. "Why did you close the door?"

"Where the hell did you come from?" Riley grabbed Blake's arm and pulled her closer to his body. "Were you just hiding in the dark, listening to us.?"

"Uh yeah, I was hiding in the dark because we're playing fucking hide-and-seek, dipshit. I wedged myself under the bunk bed, I got a bit stuck." Jasper pointed at the closed door, his expression angry. "Why did you shut the door? We're locked in here now."

Riley shook his head. "No, we enter the code, Pen's b-day, right?"

"Yeah, like a year ago." Jasper's jaw was clenched, his gaze hard. "You honestly think the code is still the same? Does that sound like the way Jace works to you? Because I'm pretty sure he changes all the fucking codes and passwords around here every few weeks."

Riley turned to a small panel beside the door, typing in an eight-digit code, frowning when the keypad beeped and turned red. "Shit." Riley tried another series of numbers, getting the same results. "Okay, so we wait until Jace can't find us and then he'll come look here. He'll take off the clothespin and know where we are."

"Now who's high?" Jasper sat on one of the bottom bunks, his head in his hands. "He's not even going to wear the damn clothespin. He's going to go find Axe and fuck her wherever she's hiding. And then he's going to toss her over his shoulder and take her to bed and fuck her some more." Jasper picked his head up, leveling his glare on Riley. "I've lived with them long enough to know exactly how this is going to go."

Blake knew why Jasper was angry, knew why he seemed to be spiraling. It wasn't lost on her Riley had locked the three of them in here together and the potential threat that could pose. "They have to come up for air at some point, right?"

"Right." Jasper nodded, meeting her gaze from across the room. "In a few hours, they'll come up for air and they'll come looking for us. But by that point, either I'll be dead in the corner, or Riley will."

No one spoke. No one knew what else to say.

Jasper was on edge, afraid of hurting her, afraid of his wolf.

Riley was rigid beside her, his every muscle tense and ready for a fight.

Blake was standing between the two of them, racking her brain to find a way to save them all.

Chapter Thirty-Four

Riley

Riley should've been paying attention to his surroundings, to the smells and sounds. He had heightened senses and he should've damn well used them. He'd been too consumed with Blake, too ready to have his mouth on her again. She was an addiction, an obsession, and it had clouded his judgment so completely he'd made a grave mistake. He'd locked them in the safe room, effectively creating the perfect environment for a cage match of epic proportions.

"Blake should be okay for a couple of hours. I wouldn't have agreed to hide-and-seek if I thought she couldn't handle it." Riley was standing in front of the couch where Blake was sitting, blocking her body from Jasper.

"Well, you've already been out of your bedroom for two hours, genius." Jasper glanced down at his watch. "How much longer you think we've got before you try to rip my throat out?"

Riley honestly didn't know. He hoped they had more time. He hoped like hell Axie and Jace would come looking for them, would let them out of here before Blake's body started to react to the unfinished bond. But there was no guarantee, was there?

Jasper was right. The potential for blood was real.

"Jasper, I'm sorry."

"Blake, you don't need to apologize." Jasper peeked around Riley's body, making eye contact with Blake. "Look, I don't mean to be so harsh, but it sucks. I hate I have the capacity to hurt you. I hate I can't seem to overrule my wolf. The loss of control, the threat of what could happen. It's heavy."

Riley felt for his friend, but his concern for Blake overrode everything else. Even his packmate's dilemma. He pulled his cell out of his pocket for the tenth time, hoping to see a bar of service pop up. He tried re-sending the same text to Jace and Axie, squeezing his phone in his palm, praying it would miraculously go through.

The three of them sat in complete silence. It seemed no one knew what to say, knew how to break the loaded potential of their situation with a joke or casual conversation.

Riley kept doing the math over and over in his head. He'd made Blake come in the shower, twice. Then they'd walked downstairs, and he'd met with Jace, and after that Jasper had suggested this game.

Had it been two hours already like Jasper said? Would Blake's body up their game, escalating—

"Fuck." Riley glanced behind him, his gaze assessing his future mate.

She looked up, meeting his gaze. "What? What's wrong?"

Riley licked his lips, his desire for her mounting with each passing second. "It's happening."

"No, I feel fine." Blake put her hands on her cheeks, her forehead, as if she was checking for a temperature. "I've been sitting here not thinking of anything sexy at all. I've been singing the states song in my head on repeat. You know…Alabama, Alaska, Arizona, Arkansas."

"No, he's right." Jasper stood, pacing the room while Riley moved to stand completely in front of Blake. Jasper pulled at his hair, and his breathing turned shallow. "The bathroom, lock yourselves in the bathroom."

Riley grabbed Blake's hand, dragging her up off the couch and across the room. He helped her step into the tub, then turned to shut the door. "Shit. There's no lock on this door." Riley pushed his back against the door, his hand on the counter to his left for extra leverage.

"Maybe the pheromones won't be as strong with the door between us." Riley met Blake's gaze, seeing the fear in her eyes. Her cheeks were flushed, her thighs pressed together. She was feeling it now, the desire for the bond overwhelming her small body.

"That door better be fucking locked, man, my wolf is losing his shit." Jasper sounded agitated, strained. Riley could picture him pacing the room, his hair standing on end, like a caged tiger.

Or wolf. A cornered wolf looking for a way out, any way out.

Riley pushed back against the door with everything he had, bracing his feet into the tiled floor. He was the only thing standing between his mate and his best friend and he wanted to be able to save them all.

There was a loud bang on the door, and Riley jerked forward. "Fuck, man, I'm sorry. Fuck. I can't. I need her." Jasper was on the other side of the thin wood, his voice sounded like he was being tortured, ripped apart from the inside.

"Just claim me." Blake stepped out of the tub, stepping closer to him, pulling her shirt over her head. "It'll stop after that, right? He'll be okay once I'm all the way yours."

Riley shook his head, jerking when Jasper's fist collided with the door again. "I'm not doing that. Not here and not like this. You deserve more. We deserve more."

"What about Jasper, what does he deserve? He's your best friend and he's out there losing his mind, suffering, terrified of himself and what he's capable of." Blake was crying, silent tears running down her gorgeous face. "I don't need candles and flowers, Riley. That's not the girl I am. I need you to be okay, I need Jasper to be okay. I care more about the two of you than I do myself. Please. Finish this."

Riley closed his eyes, letting his head fall back against the door. Blake was putting the pack before herself. He loved her, there was no denying that. He wanted her. He wanted to claim her as his own and spend the rest of his life making sure she was happy and cherished. He wanted to give her everything she deserved. He wanted to make their bonding special.

But… Maybe this was the way it was always supposed to be. His wolf claiming his forever while Jasper's watched. Wasn't that what Jasper said in Jace's office? His wolf needed closure, to bear witness.

This was the ultimate closure.

Riley opened his eyes, taking in the beautiful girl standing shirtless in front of him. Her blue eyes were bright from her tears and her skin had a pink tint from the flush taking over her perfect body. Her curls were down, resting over her chest and across her back. She looked so fucking perfect. "Do you trust me?"

"Yes," she answered without hesitation, her belief in him and his intentions shining through her small smile.

"Jasper, man, back away from the door." Riley sighed, taking a moment to calm his racing heart. "I'm going to bring her out, I'm going to let you see her."

Riley opened the door slowly, taking Blake's hand and pulling her out into the open space but keeping her firmly behind him. Jasper was crouched down, his back against the side of the couch and his head once again in his hands. He looked tortured as he rose to his feet, making a beeline right for them.

Riley threw out his hand. "No." He stood his ground, keeping his body between Jasper's and Blake's. "You can't touch her. If you try to touch her, I will kill you." Jasper stopped short, panting with his hands clenched into tight fists at his sides. "Do you understand that? Do you understand I will rip your throat out? I *will* kill you. You'll be dead. Gone forever. Blake will be sad. It'll make her hurt. She'll be upset for a long, long time."

Jasper cocked his head to the side, his gaze on Blake, like he was studying her to see if there was truth to Riley's words. After a few tense moments, Jasper's shoulders lowered, he hands went lax. He nodded but didn't speak.

Riley hoped he wasn't making the wrong choice. He hoped like hell he was right in thinking that Jasper's wolf wouldn't want to make Blake hurt. It made sense. It was instinct. She was a female in his pack, and he'd protect her to the ends of the earth. He didn't care about his own life, not when he was so focused on having Blake for himself. Turning it around, explaining his actions would cause her pain was the only play Riley had left.

He pointed toward the small kitchen table. "Get that chair, bring it in here and put it by that bed. Not too close."

Riley used his hold on Blake's hand to bring her around in front of him, putting his palms on her blushing cheeks. "It's going to be okay, doll face. I'll never let anyone hurt you, ever. You're my girl, you're mine to love and cherish and protect until I take my last breath."

Blake rested her forehead against his, whispering against his lips. "I think I've loved you since the moment I first saw you. I was drawn to you. I was compelled to know you, to make you smile, to make you live."

"I'll spend the rest of my life making sure that you never regret this choice, not for one single second." Riley glanced over this shoulder, seeing Jasper sitting in the kitchen chair, his eyes on them. He didn't look so crazed anymore, his expression curious, full of anticipation. "I wish I could do this differently. I wish I could give you what you deserve."

"This is the way it's supposed to be." Blake leaned in, swiping her tongue across the seam of his lips. "And that's more than okay."

Riley kissed her, pouring his love, his devotion into her. He pressed her down onto the small twin-size bunk mattress, devouring the soft moans coming from her mouth. He could sense Jasper a few feet away, could feel his eyes on them. There was no menace in the air, no threat of violence. Jasper's wolf understood what was happening, understood she wasn't for him and he couldn't touch her.

Riley couldn't give her the experience he wanted. He couldn't take his time and worship every inch of her body. He hated that, but at the same time he understood he had the rest of forever to take her nice and slow, make love to her for hours on end, night after night.

Blake's hands went to his zipper, pushing his jeans down enough to free his hard cock. He'd been aching for her for days, wanting desperately to bury himself inside her again. He ripped through her yoga pants, not wanting to expose too much of her flesh to the wolf watching them. He rained kisses on her collarbone, the side of her neck. "Keep your eyes open, watch me."

Blake nodded, her fingers digging into his scalp, her hips grinding up to meet his. "I'm ready, please, Riley…" His name on her lips spurred him forward: he thrusted into her in one fluid movement. He paused, filling his mate, taking a moment to appreciate how fucking perfect she felt wrapped around him.

Her gaze moved past him for a moment, watching Jasper while he watched them. Riley nuzzled her neck, licking her flesh and savoring the sweet taste of her skin. He moved inside her, one of his hands on her throat, the other on her thigh, hiking it farther up his hip to open her even more. His wolf demanded he bury himself as deep as possible, but he kept his thrusts shallow, not wanting to leave her body, even a fraction of an inch. "Now look at me, doll."

He waited until her pretty blue eyes met his before he started pounding into her. He wanted to claim her, bond her to him for the rest of time. Then wanted to get her the fuck out of this room. His wolf didn't love that Jasper was there, watching this sacred thing between them, but he wasn't mad about it either.

"Fuck, Riley, don't stop." She bit at her bottom lip, her nails dragging down his back and digging into his ass, demanding even more. "I'm so close."

He palmed her face, holding her gaze as he buried himself deep inside her. Her core tightened, holding him hostage, milking his orgasm from his body while she came with his name on her lips.

The air seemed to shimmer around them, their surroundings nothing but a blur for a few moments.

Then his world dropped back into focus, his heart so completely full of love for the girl clinging to him.

Chapter Thirty-Five

Riley

Blake was asleep in his arms. He'd pulled the blankets up over them. Her head was on his chest and his hand was behind his head. She was his now forever. They belonged to each other. The tension, the jealousy he'd been feeling over the last week was nonexistent. His heart was whole, and he knew no one would ever be able to take her away from him. He turned his head toward the small living area where Jasper was lying on the couch, his arm thrown over his eyes. "You feel better?"

Jasper nodded. "I feel lighter. My wolf is calm, content."

Jasper's feelings mirrored Riley's in a lot of ways. Everything was as it should be, and everyone could relax now.

"This won't happen again. You know that, right? She isn't ours, she's mine. Forever." He'd allowed Jasper to watch out of necessity, out of preservation for them all. He wouldn't allow it again though.

"I know she's yours. So does my wolf. We see her like we see Axie. We love her. We'd die for her. But we don't desire her." Jasper sat up, his feet on the ground. "Maybe it was always supposed to be this way. We've shared so much over the years. I don't know if my wolf would have fully accepted our bond was broken unless he witnessed it himself. Blake becoming yours, you becoming only hers."

Riley shook his head. "Our bond isn't broken, man. We're pack. We're family."

Blake was his and he in turn was hers. That didn't mean his bond with Jasper was any weaker. He saw that now. It was altered, sure. But not broken.

The silence was suddenly breached by the sound of the locked door whooshing open. "What in the actual fuck? How did the three of you end up in this clusterfuck?" Jace stepped into the room, his hands on his hips, his gaze assessing the scene in front of him.

Riley carefully untangled himself from his sleeping mate, not wanting to wake her. The drama and the claiming had seemed to exhaust her. "Jasper was hiding in here already. I didn't know. I brought Blake in here and shut the door. You changed the code. Chaos ensued, I had to finish the bond to keep us from killing each other." A somewhat brief synopsis for a really fucking monumental two hours.

Jace's gaze moved to the nearly destroyed bathroom door. There were holes in the wood where Jasper had hit it. "There's no lock on that door."

Jasper snorted. "No shit, bro."

Jace pointed to the other side of the room. "Why didn't you use the other bedroom?" All heads turned to the second closed door none of them had seemed to notice in the chaos. "It has a nicer bed and a deadbolt on the door."

Chapter Thirty-Six

Blake

The guys had been holed up in Jace's office for the past few hours, glued to all the security monitors around the property and the houses where their packmates lived in town. Jace sent the information on the man who tried to threaten her life, and all they could do now was wait for the authorities to do their job. She was in awe of the way they protected each other, the way they refused to allow anyone they cared about to get hurt.

Blake'd had a nice dinner with Axie, and she'd told Blake more about what she, Jace, and Jasper had been doing over the last few months. They'd helped send so many criminals to jail. They'd made the world a better place. It was selfless, really, to put so much time and effort in to stop bad things before they even had a chance to happen.

Constantine, the one who'd been tracking the pack, sending the pictures and threats? He was pure evil. Drugs, guns, human trafficking—he had a hand in every piece of the pie. He was a dangerous man. Blake hadn't realized how serious the threat on her life really was. Her love and appreciation for the pack grew. After dinner she'd gone upstairs to shower and decompress.

"Claimed by her shifter" was a phrase she would've never believed she'd ever think, never mind do. She was connected to Riley forever. They were destined to live and love until the end of their time here on earth. It was a big thought, but she'd never been overwhelmed by it. To be honest, Blake found the drama of it fitting.

"It's done. He was picked up thirty minutes ago by the FBI." Riley came into their bedroom, pulling his shirt over his head and tossing it to the floor. "We can go back to Greenly tomorrow. Get ready for the spring semester."

Blake ran her fingers through his messy red hair when he laid his head in her lap. "How do mates work when they live in separate resident buildings? I have a roommate."

Riley pulled a key out his pocket, holding it up so it caught the lamplight beside them. "Jace bought an investment property. He intended for Jasper and me to live in it while we're in school. But now, it's your home too."

Blake took the key, squeezing it in her palm. "Freshmen have to live on campus."

"Nah, Jace took care of that too."

"How?"

Riley shrugged. "When it comes to Jace and his ways, it's best not to ask too many questions, doll face."

Blake laughed, handing the key back to Riley for safekeeping. "How am I supposed to explain any of this to my parents? Hey, Mom and Dad, this is my boyfriend Riley, he turns into a wolf, and I live with him and his BFF Jasper." She rolled her eyes. "Their brains will melt and stain the expensive carpets I'm sure Jace furnished the house with."

"First of all, I'm not your boyfriend. I'm your mate." Riley grabbed Blake's hands, putting them back into his hair. "Second of all, your parents don't need to know I shift, or that my bff does either. You can keep your dorm room for the rest of the year. You can meet them there when they come to visit."

"Okay, but how do I tell them that I'm basically the human version of married? You haven't even met them yet, and there's no ring or ceremony. No reception for my cousins to get shitfaced at. They won't understand any of this."

Riley rolled over and sat up. "I guess it's been a long time since someone mated into the pack with a family of humans." He cupped her cheeks, kissing her lips in a way that made her swoon. "We'll let them watch us 'date' for the rest of the year, then over the summer we'll tell them we're moving in together. Then I'll stage an engagement in a couple years and we'll have a big party. Your family can drink until they pass out. Or…"

She narrowed her eyes at his sexy smirk. "Or what?"

"I knock you up and we rush a shotgun wedding." He waggled his eyebrows, rising up over her and pushing her back into the mattress, settling between her thighs. "Much simpler."

"You been smoking Jasper's weed?" He kissed her again, his hand slipping into the waistband of her pajama pants. "I want to finish school before I birth a litter of babies."

"Better not miss one of those pills then, because I plan on coming inside this perfect pussy every fucking chance I get."

Her core reacted to Riley's words as if they'd been spoken with his tongue against her clit. "How is it possible you've gotten more possessive and hornier after the claiming? I thought it was supposed to be the other way around."

His fingers slipped inside her heat, his hips grinding with his movements. "I'll never be able to get enough of you, doll face, fucking never." His wolf claimed what was his, again and again, until the sun began to turn the sky from inky black to a deep purple.

Chapter Thirty-Seven

Riley

Riley left Blake upstairs, asleep in bed. They'd come together over and over, all night long. He'd meant what he'd told her, he'd never get enough of her. Jasper had to drag him out of bed and down into Jace's office. Baze was there too, standing by the window, his arms crossed over his chest.

"You guys are free to head back to campus. We have pack dinner tonight, but after that, you can go whenever you're ready." Jace stood next to Baze, never one to sit down when his alpha was standing at attention.

Riley, Jasper, and Blake would load up the truck and make the drive back to the house near campus. Riley would need to hide where he was staying from his coaches. Being a student athlete, he was supposed to live on campus. He'd break every rule in the handbook if it meant he got to fall asleep beside his mate every night.

"So what happens to this one? How long will he be in jail?" Jasper clasped his hands behind his head, his eyes on his brother.

"Locked up, awaiting trial. The FBI said the evidence is irrefutable." Jace nodded, dark circles under his eyes giving away how much stress the last six months had caused him. He acted and looked so much older than his twenty years. "Feds have brought in eyewitnesses who we'd handed them. He'll go away for life."

"Okay, then why do you still look like someone just told you getting head causes male pattern baldness?" Jasper jerked his chin up. "What gives, twin bro?" It seemed Riley wasn't the only one who'd noticed how exhausted Jace looked these days.

Jace sighed, his shoulders slumping in a rare display of defeat. "I'm starting to think we were naïve, crazy even, to think that this plan of ours would work." He sat in the chair behind his desk, a rare occurrence, which pointed to how unwell Jace was. Sitting when Baze was still standing? Never happened.

"What do you mean? Jace, man, you've rid the world of so much fucking evil over the last six months." Riley, the whole pack, they owed Jace a huge debt. "You've saved countless lives. Screw Mathias, you're the actual Avenger."

Matias had compared himself to Robin Hood. Corey had taken his bravado and had run with it, likening him to Thor. Mathias was a badass, there was no denying that. His computer skills, his mercenary killer vibes, they'd all been a huge asset. However, it was Jace who'd decided to take on the underworld and devote his life to their pack's safety, to their continued survival.

"I made a small dent in a large tank." Jace shook his head. "What happens when the next round of scum decides to rise up, take over, wreak havoc?"

"Don't borrow trouble, kid," Baze said, clearly trying to pull Jace out of his funk.

Jace scoffed. "It'll never be over. It'll never be the end. There's no shortage of evil people in this world, we all know that. Monsters are born and bred every day. Hell, I was meant to be the second generation of Franklin's empire. You think our asshole of a sperm donor was the only bad guy who sired kids?"

Damn. Riley woke up in an excellent mood and Jace was really bringing the whole vibe of the house down. He knew that so much rested on his beta's shoulders, he wished he could snap his fingers and give Jace the easy life he deserved. The easy life he'd earned.

"Then we become the biggest monster of them all." All four male gazes flew to the door when Axie spoke up. How long had she been standing there? For sure, she'd picked up some of Jace's covert op stealth skills.

"Baby, that's—"

"We keep watch, and we never stop taking out the monsters." She stepped into the room, moving to stand behind her mate, her small hands on his broad shoulders. "Who needs college, who needs a nine-to-five?" Her smile was wicked. "We're good at beating evil men at their own game. We've both been doing it since we were old enough to talk. Why stop now?"

Jace took his mate's hand, placing a kiss to her palm. "Why stop now."

Chapter Thirty-Eight

Riley

Three Months Later

"Soundproofing our bedrooms is probably the best idea Jasper has ever had." Riley grinned up at his mate where she was perched on his dick, her blonde hair a mess from his hands pulling at the curls as she rode him. "That was ego-stroking loud, doll face."

She laughed as she leaned down and kissed his lips, then hopped off him and headed into the bathroom to clean up. He refused to pull out, and he refused condoms. His wolf wouldn't let him come anywhere other than inside her. He knew neither he nor Blake was ready to be parents, but he looked forward to the day she threw her birth control in the trash so they could start a family. He wanted tiny blonde clones of his girl. Hilariously dramatic and loyal-to-no-end kids.

He, Blake, and Jasper had been living together for three months and it'd been going better than he could've ever imagined. The was no jealousy, no fear of wanting to hurt his best friend for being close friends with his mate. They seemed to have reached the perfect balance of pack and family. They ate dinner together every night and had movie marathons on the couch.

If Riley wasn't available to walk Blake to class, Jasper jumped in to make sure she was safe. Blake went to all their games. Hell, she was the one who encouraged Jasper to go after his walk-on spot on the team. She was their biggest supporter.

"Anyone naked?" Jasper knocked, opening their bedroom door with his hand over his eyes. "Not that I haven't seen it all before."

Riley grabbed a pillow from behind him and launched it at his best friend. "Hilarious."

"I thought so." Jasper perched on the edge of their bed, high-fiving Blake when she came out of the bathroom dressed in her jeans and cropped t-shirt. "We partying tonight? It's our one free weekend until baseball season is over."

Riley groaned, looking across the room to his open laptop with the cursor blinking on the blank page. "I have to write a paper that needs to be turned in by midnight."

"Then it's you and me. You game?" Jasper grabbed her by the hips and tossed her up the bed toward Riley. "We can get some drinks and you can play wingman. There's this sweet quiet chick from my lit class I've been itching to corrupt."

Blake wrinkled her nose. "Callahan? The chick with the glasses and the freckles?" When Jasper nodded, licking his lips, she threw her head back, laughing. "You realize you're going after a sweet, quiet redhead, right?"

"So?" Jasper frowned, seemingly confused by her laughter.

"Your sweet, quiet best friend got all mated up and won't let you see his dick anymore, so you're replacing him with a female version." Blake giggled.

"Why are you so obsessed with me, bro?" Riley couldn't help but join his mate, and he honestly saw a little bit of truth in what she was saying.

Jasper rolled his eyes and climbed off the bed. "You two suck." He put his hands on his hips, scowling at a still-laughing Blake. "You coming with or not?"

"Oh, I'm not about to miss this." She straddled Riley once again, kissing him deeply before hopping up and letting Jasper throw her over his shoulder. "I'll come back home as soon as she turns him down, sourpuss."

Jasper spun around, nearly knocking Blake's head into the doorframe. "I'll drop her ass back home on my way to seal the deal."

"Have fun." Riley got up, fighting the desire to shut off his computer and go with them. "Love you."

Both Jasper and Blake screamed it back.

Riley wasn't sure what the other males in his pack would think about the relationship between Blake and Jasper, the ease and comfort between them. It wasn't conventional. Most males would hate anyone else touching their mate, being in their space, and spending time alone with them. It worked though, the bond between Jasper, Blake, and Riley. He assumed it was because of the way they'd started. Or maybe it was the way the bonding had been completed with Jasper there, almost a part of it.

In the end, it didn't really matter what anyone else thought. Riley had his best friend and his mate, and he got to keep them both.

He got to watch them love each other.

UP NEXT, JASPER'S STORY
Mind Blowing

PLAYLIST

Violent – Carolesdaughter
Angry Too – Lola Blanc
Crush – Tessa Violet
Tomorrow Never Knows – Alison Mosshart & Carla Azar
Heather – Conan Grey
Lights On – The Pierces
Recess – Melanie Martinez
People I Don't Like – UPSAHL
All I Want – Kodaline
Panic Room – Au/Ra
Once Upon A Dream – Lana Del Ray
I Don't Know My Name – Grace VanderWaal
Joke's On You – Charlotte Lawrence
Merry Happy – Kate Nash

ABOUT THE AUTHOR

L.P. lives in Austin, Texas with her husband, two daughters, two dogs, and a plant-killing cat.

Writer, business owner, and office manager, L.P. says she loves to read as much as she loves to write. Reading a good book is her reward after writing one. In her spare time—ha!—she fosters puppies for a rescue organization based in Austin.

Connect with L.P.:
Website: www.lpmaxa.com
IG: @lpmaxa
Twitter: @lpmaxa
FB: pages/LP-Maxa/1442560722667127

www.BOROUGHSPUBLISHINGGROUP.com

If you enjoyed this book, please write a review. Our authors appreciate the feedback, and it helps future readers find books they love. We welcome your comments and invite you to send them to info@boroughspublishinggroup.com. Follow us on Facebook, Twitter and Instagram, and be sure to sign up for our newsletter for surprises and new releases from your favorite authors.

Are you an aspiring writer? Check out www.boroughspublishinggroup.com/submit and see if we can help you make your dreams come true.

www.ingramcontent.com/pod-product-compliance
Lightning Source LLC
Chambersburg PA
CBHW031347170626
46807CB00002B/861